The Promise of
Surrender

Also From Liliana Hart

THE MACKENZIE SERIES
Dane
A Christmas Wish: Dane
Thomas
To Catch A Cupid: Thomas
Riley
Fireworks: Riley
Cooper
A MacKenzie Christmas
MacKenzie Box Set
Cade
Shadows and Silk
Secrets and Satin
Sins and Scarlet Lace
The MacKenzie Security Series *(Includes the 3 books listed above)*
1001 Dark Nights: Captured in Surrender
Sizzle
Crave

THE COLLECTIVE SERIES
Kill Shot

THE RENA DRAKE SERIES
Breath of Fire

ADDISON HOLMES MYSTERIES
Whiskey Rebellion
Whiskey Sour
Whiskey For Breakfast
Whiskey, You're The Devil

The Promise of Surrender
A MacKenzie Family Novella
By Liliana Hart

1001 Dark Nights

EVIL EYE
CONCEPTS

The Promise of Surrender
A MacKenzie Family Novella
By Liliana Hart

1001 Dark Nights

Copyright 2015 Liliana Hart
ISBN: 978-1-940887-79-1

Foreword: Copyright 2014 M. J. Rose

Published by Evil Eye Concepts, Incorporated

Acknowledgments

To Scott,

I'm glad I married you. Even though you jumped out of the closet and scared me.

Sign up for the 1001 Dark Nights Newsletter
and be entered to win a Tiffany Key necklace.

There's a contest every month!

Go to www.1001DarkNights.com to subscribe.

As a bonus, all subscribers will receive a free
1001 Dark Nights story
The First Night
by Lexi Blake & M.J. Rose

One Thousand And One Dark Nights

Once upon a time, in the future…

*I was a student fascinated with stories and learning.
I studied philosophy, poetry, history, the occult, and
the art and science of love and magic. I had a vast
library at my father's home and collected thousands
of volumes of fantastic tales.*

*I learned all about ancient races and bygone
times. About myths and legends and dreams of all
people through the millennium. And the more I read
the stronger my imagination grew until I discovered
that I was able to travel into the stories… to actually
become part of them.*

*I wish I could say that I listened to my teacher
and respected my gift, as I ought to have. If I had, I
would not be telling you this tale now.
But I was foolhardy and confused, showing off
with bravery.*

*One afternoon, curious about the myth of the
Arabian Nights, I traveled back to ancient Persia to
see for myself if it was true that every day Shahryar
(Persian: شهريار, "king") married a new virgin, and then
sent yesterday's wife to be beheaded. It was written
and I had read, that by the time he met Scheherazade,
the vizier's daughter, he'd killed one thousand
women.*

Something went wrong with my efforts. I arrived in the midst of the story and somehow exchanged places with Scheherazade – a phenomena that had never occurred before and that still to this day, I cannot explain.

Now I am trapped in that ancient past. I have taken on Scheherazade's life and the only way I can protect myself and stay alive is to do what she did to protect herself and stay alive.

Every night the King calls for me and listens as I spin tales. And when the evening ends and dawn breaks, I stop at a point that leaves him breathless and yearning for more. And so the King spares my life for one more day, so that he might hear the rest of my dark tale.

As soon as I finish a story... I begin a new one... like the one that you, dear reader, have before you now.

Chapter One

She had him pegged for a cop the second he stepped out of the beat-up pickup truck.

He opened the back of the cab and pulled out a cardboard box, maybe a foot long and wide. His worn sneakers scuffed against the graveled parking lot, and even through the surveillance cameras that covered every square inch of her property, she could see the outline of his backup weapon strapped to his ankle.

"Lord, save me from rookies." Mia stopped processing her inventory to watch him out of curiosity. She'd spent the weekend at an estate sale and ended up with more boxes than she'd planned. That was usually how it went, but she had a knack for things that would sell for a profit.

The guy was tall and thin as a rail, his hair long and shaggy, and he had a partial growth of beard on his face. She could see why they'd want him for undercover work. He had the naturally too-thin build that made him able to pass for a junkie. He was just a baby, maybe a year or two out of the academy, and he had no idea the toll that working undercover would have on his life.

"Get out while you still can, boy." She shook her head sadly.

There was no warning them—the rookies. They thought working undercover was like it was on TV—sexy and dangerous—living life on the edge between good and evil. And then six months into the job they realized it wasn't so sexy, but it sure as hell was dangerous. They were lying to spouses and family and friends, living a double life, and they were doing things the soul would never be able to reconcile. All for the greater good.

His jeans and T-shirt looked like he'd gotten them straight from a thrift store and he wasn't quite comfortable in them. He was used to being pressed and polished. A silver-spoon kid. He'd probably been a patrolman, used to the uniform, and the dead giveaway was the way he kept tapping his elbow against his side, checking for his duty weapon.

He walked like a cop. And his eyes scanned the area like a cop—like he was trying to see where his backup was located just in case he needed a rescue. Surely working undercover hadn't changed that much in the last ten years. This guy was lucky to be alive if his commander was sending him out with that much green on him.

Mia wasn't the most patient of people on her best days. And today wasn't one of her best days. It was barely noon, and a variety of customers had already come into the shop. Each one had made her head pound a little harder.

She'd opened Pawn to Queen six years before with nothing but sweat, blood, and the money she'd taken in one lump sum from her pension. There'd been no rhyme or reason as to why she'd picked Surrender, Montana. Not that she wasn't familiar with the area and all the little towns that dotted the Montana landscape like pictures on a postcard. But there'd been something about Surrender that had called to her to make it home.

Even with the appeal of the rolling hills, white fences, and the shops downtown with matching black awnings and flowers placed along the wooden walkways, she knew she couldn't sully the peaceful image of the town with her shop. She'd never fooled herself into thinking her clientele was a cut above all the other pawnshop owners out there. For the most part, she was dealing with the dregs of humanity. So she'd built her shop on the outskirts of town, just outside the city limits on the other side of the hill.

Surrender was unique in that it was located at the base of several large hills, nestled like a little green jewel in the valley. Any direction visitors came from, the exits led to one main road, up and over the hill, so when they reached the top there was a crystal clear view of the little town tucked below—the *Welcome to Surrender* sign gleaming a bright and polished green at the summit.

Mia lived in a pretty little apartment above the bakery. It was painted white and had beveled windows and a spindled railing along the balcony. Smells of cinnamon rolls and fresh baked bread wafted up through the vents each morning. She was still considered an outsider, though people were friendly when she did her weekly grocery shopping or stopped to grab a bite to eat at the diner. They were friendly—but wary.

The people in Surrender came from a different era. The men were rugged and muscled from working the ranches. The denim of their jeans worn at the knees and back pockets, their boots scuffed and comfortable from use. The ranch women were as sturdy as their men, and they all worked like dogs to preserve a heritage that would go to their own children. Ranching was harsh, but it provided a good life.

The town ladies—at least that's what Mia liked to call them—were a whole different story. It was almost comical the way they scurried about from shop to shop, gossiping more than attending to errands. It was their pastime and they made no apologies about enjoying it immensely.

They'd start the day at the bakery, then take their recyclable shopping bags over to the mercantile. They'd eventually wander to the bookstore, the florist, and a little place that only sold honey and homemade candles made of beeswax, visiting with the shop owners and catching up on any news they might have missed—engagements, new babies, whose cows got loose and caused a ruckus, or who got drunk and disorderly down at Duffey's Pub the night before—all news was met with equal excitement.

There was a clothing boutique for ladies owned by Annabeth MacKenzie, but it didn't exactly cater to the kinds of things Mia liked to wear, though Annabeth was very sweet, if a little shy. Next door to Annabeth's shop was a clothing store for men that carried the hardy clothes for ranch life—Wranglers, Stetsons, and boots. There was a feed store next to that, an ice cream parlor, and the bakery occupied the corner building.

There was always some kind of ladies club meeting happening one place or another. Casserole recipes were doled out like gold bullion, and they all dressed like every day was Sunday.

Mia was a puzzlement to the women in town. She didn't talk about herself, though she was always friendly when they spoke to her. But she'd had a lot of practice avoiding invasive questions, so she smiled and turned the conversation around so she wasn't the focus.

She'd had to fill out a background check when she'd rented the little apartment, but law enforcement records didn't show on a standard check. All they knew was that her name was Mia Marie Russo and she was a thirty-four-year-old female with no family and no criminal history. And it hadn't hurt that she'd been able to pay six months rent up front.

Her landlady had been disappointed at the lack of news to carry on to her friends. It wasn't every day a single woman with a sleeve of tattoos and purple streaks in her hair moved to Surrender. And it wasn't every day that same woman built a pawnshop on the outskirts of town and carried a visible weapon everywhere she went.

Mia had built her shop just after the exit at the base of the other side of the hill, away from the pristine beauty of

Surrender. She'd picked the perfect location. It was nothing but open land—no trees or hills or valleys. With the amount of cash and valuable inventory she often had on hand, it was best not to give people available hiding places.

A long, rectangular cabin with a metal roof had given her the most efficient space for the best price, and it was surrounded by a graveled parking lot. In a year or two she'd be able to afford to have it paved. She'd had bars installed on the windows for extra security and the door at the back of the cabin was solid steel and bolted tight unless she was unloading a shipment or leaving or entering the premises. Her front door was always locked and customers had to be buzzed in. She was always armed. Which she was grateful for after the customers she'd already dealt with that morning.

Her first customer of the day had been an addict trying to pawn what looked like family heirlooms. He'd probably stolen them from his own mother, as he'd seemed familiar with each piece. She'd lowballed him, hoping he'd reject the offer, but he'd taken the cash with shaky hands and a gleam in his eye that told her he was already focused on his next fix. She entered the information into the online database, put the heirlooms in an envelope, and stuck them in the safe beneath her register. Maybe someone would come in looking to get them back.

Her second customer had been a woman on the verge of a breakdown. The woman carried a baby in a sling around her chest and held a toddler by his chubby hand. Mia had listened with a pounding headache while the woman sobbed out a story of betrayal about her no-good husband. And in the end, she'd given the woman a little more than she should have for the wedding ring set. Everyone deserved a fresh start.

Her third customer had been a big brute of a man, decked out in Vaquero biker colors and 1% patches. He'd parked his Harley sideways in front of the steps that led up to the door, and she'd felt the reverberation of his footsteps as he made his way onto the porch and hit the buzzer multiple times. She debated whether or not to let him inside. It was the reason she'd had the system installed in the first place and the cameras in the lot. It was her business. Her terms.

Her gun was holstered at her waist and her right hand rested comfortably on the sawed off she kept beneath the counter. She flicked the button to release the door latch and allowed him entry. Each step he took shook the floor-to-ceiling metal shelves.

Her display counter was three sides of a big square—the fourth storeroom. Her register was centered in the middle of the square so no one could reach over the counter and take money. Her customers didn't know it, but she'd invested in bulletproof glass to protect the more expensive items she kept in the display counter.

Biker dude pressed his palms down on the glass and stared her down. She'd been stared down by worse than him, so she just stared back.

"Can I help you?" she finally asked.

"I believe you have something of mine. It's a music box. Very old. Wooden. And when you open it and wind it up you can see all the workings on the inside."

"You've lost an antique music box?" she asked skeptically.

"It was my mother's," he lied easily. "I was told it was brought here and you paid someone for it. I'll give you double what you paid."

"That's very generous of you, but the only music boxes I have are sitting on the shelf over there. You're welcome to check them out."

His jaw clenched and his smile sent chills up her spine. "Maybe you forgot you bought it," he said. "So I'm going to ask you one more time." He pressed against the counter and leaned forward until his face was inches from hers. "Go get the music box from the back."

He couldn't mistake the sound of her cocking the shotgun, and his brown eyes narrowed with malice. "Like I've already said. I haven't acquired any music boxes recently. Maybe check down the road at *Pawn and Go* in Myrna Springs."

Her voice was calm, but her heart hammered in her chest. She'd have to be fast if things went to shit. If it weren't for the bulletproof counters, she could've pulled the trigger and shot straight through. But she knew in her gut there was no way she could be fast enough to pull the shotgun out, aim, and fire. She'd let him get in too close. Her mistake, and she knew better. Civilian life had made her soft.

She stared him down with nothing but bluster, and to her surprise, he took a step back and dropped his hands down to his side.

"Why don't you keep an eye out for that music box? My brothers and I will come back for a visit soon. Real soon."

He left the shop, the door banging shut behind him, and she breathed out a sigh of relief.

"Perfect. Now I've got an entire outlaw motorcycle club to deal with. Must be my lucky day."

Mia went to the front door and made sure the latch was closed tight, and then she went into her office and unlocked the bottom drawer of her desk. Inside it sat the wooden music box she'd bought from Tina Wolfe the day before. She'd given her a hundred bucks for it and the woman had gladly taken it.

Mia wasn't one to judge—she dealt with people from all walks of life—and she knew that sometimes life dealt one shitty hand after another. That's the impression she'd gotten from Tina. She was a woman who looked like she'd ridden a hard road. Her license placed her at twenty-six, but Mia would've guessed a hard forty. A combination of the sun, alcohol, and the smoke that reeked from her clothing had aged her face considerably.

She'd ridden in on a nice Harley and she'd dressed the part. But there'd been a look of weariness on her face Mia found impossible to ignore. And when she looked a little closer, there was also an edge of fear. Tina was running from something or someone, and whatever cash she could get on her way was how she was going to survive.

So Mia had given her the cash and taken the music box. It was a nice piece. Early 1940s and in good shape. And the music still played crystal clear and she watched, fascinated, as the intricate wheels and cogs played *You Are My Sunshine*. It was a piece that caught her interest enough that she'd decided to take it home. Though now she had to wonder what there was about it that made the biker want it so badly.

She'd moved it to a safe location and grabbed a couple of the estate boxes from the storeroom, moving them to the front counter so she could start documenting the new inventory. Less than twenty minutes later, she'd looked up to see the rookie cop in her parking lot.

He buzzed her door, box in hand, and had a smirk on his face. She'd had about enough of people for the day. The easiest thing to do would be to let him keep buzzing and slip out the back for an early lunch. But he'd be back. He seemed determined.

Mia knew people. She knew how to read them and she knew how to fuck with them. It was all part of the job description—former and current. So she hit the buzzer and released the locks on the door. And then she barely glanced at him as he walked toward the counter. Just a quick look and an arched eyebrow. And then she dismissed him as nothing special and went back to the inventory she'd been cataloguing before bikers and cops had started overrunning her shop.

The box landed with a light thump next to her and he waited a few seconds in silence. His fingers drummed against the counter and he cleared his throat. She tried to hide her smile.

"What am I invisible?" he said. He wasn't from around this area judging by the accent. Maybe Chicago, if she had to guess.

He was easily summed up. Hot head. Thought he was too good for the job and God's gift to police. His badge was still shiny and new and he'd moved from the big city to Montana, where none of the departments were very big outside of the major cities. The only reason a man made that big of a change was for a woman or so he could start over. This guy didn't look like the kind of man who'd do anything for a woman, so she was guessing door number two.

He wouldn't last a month working undercover in this territory. Drugs were a huge problem, and the agents working u/c were used to the terrain—running suspects to ground across mountains and rivers—facing drug cartels one night and the outlaw motorcycle clubs the next. Manpower was short and physical characteristics determined the job more than ability—if you looked like a crackhead or a meth dealer you worked ops completely different than if you had the build of a biker.

She'd been neither. She'd always looked younger than her age and she'd ended up in various high schools across the state, looking for whoever was supplying the kids with drugs. It was a job that had been finite. She couldn't look eighteen forever.

"I'm talkin' to you, lady. Can you take a look at this? I'm in a hurry."

"Everyone looking for fast cash usually is," Mia said. "Give me a second. I'm almost done."

"You don't seem very concerned about customer service."

"You're the one trying to get cash from me. I don't have to be concerned about customer service. There are other pawnshops. You're welcome to go there."

She could practically hear his teeth grinding together and decided she might as well see what he wanted and get him out of her shop. With the clientele she usually catered to, she wasn't the only one who'd be able to sniff him out as a cop.

The sigh that escaped her lips was genuine and filled with annoyance. She dropped her pen and moved over, never looking at him directly. The inattention seemed to really bother him, so that meant he was something of a glory hound as well. It wasn't often she felt instant dislike for someone, especially another cop, but this guy rubbed her the wrong way.

"Take your stuff out of the box and set it on the

counter."

He did as she asked and she crossed her arms over her chest, wincing as he jostled it with a heavy hand before setting it clumsily on the counter.

Mia had never been accused of being a bad poker player. Her life had depended on her reactions more times than she could count. But to say that she wasn't surprised would've been a lie.

A wooden music box, identical to the one she'd held in her hands only moments before, sat in front of her. She pulled a pair of latex gloves from under the counter and slipped them on before opening the top of the music box.

It was in excellent condition, and even the green felt on the inside had similar age spots to the other. She wound it up from the bottom and the cogs and wheels began turning as *You Are My Sunshine* played. She ran her fingers around the edges and all but took it apart, looking for the tiny stamp mark that authenticated it. But it didn't have one. Because it was a fake.

"It's a nice piece," she said as if she'd never seen one like it. "I'll give you ten bucks for it."

He sputtered, "Ten bucks? Are you fucking crazy? It's gotta be worth at least a hundred and fifty. It's an antique."

"What's your name?" she asked.

He hesitated a couple of seconds before answering. "Walker Barnes."

"Uh huh," Mia said, raising her eyebrows skeptically. "Well, Walker Barnes, what you have here is a fake. If this thing was made before last week I'd be surprised."

"I think you're mistaken. Why don't you look again."

"You're the second person who's told me that in the last hour. It's as irritating now as it was then. I don't make mistakes. Look how new all the metal is. It's shiny as a copper penny. And thin. They don't make things the way they used to."

"Shit," he said, running his fingers through his hair. "Listen, I'm in a bind here. I really need to find a box just like this one that's real. Do you have one?"

Mia arched a brow. Now things were getting interesting. The cops were looking for the same music box as the biker. The question was why.

"Yeah, because I always keep identical merchandise sitting in my storeroom just for occasions such as this."

"No need to be a bitch about it."

"You're wasting my time. One of us needs to get back to work. And in case you were wondering, that would be me."

"Look, my girlfriend really loves this music box, but I don't want her to find out it was a fake. Where can I get a real one?" he asked, taking a different approach.

"Your girlfriend likes it so much you decided to come in and sell it?"

Barnes flushed red. "No, I was just thinking if it was worth something I could trade it in to get her something a little nicer. She likes jewelry too."

"Can't help you. Ten bucks. That's my offer."

"Listen, I had a friend who said you can get all kinds of stuff. That you've got connections all over the place."

"What friend would that be?" she asked.

Barnes smirked. "He likes to stay under the radar. But he assures me that you can 'get' things for people."

"I get what I know I can sell or what interests me. You have nothing I want to sell and you don't interest me. So feel free to buy something or leave."

"So is it true?" he continued. "I might have a few things I want you to look for that went missing. I know a couple people who could help retrieve them if you can find them. Maybe we can work out a deal."

Mia was done with the charade, and her blood was boiling at the thought that they'd come in and try to...*test* her. That was the only way she could really describe how it felt. As if she were auditioning for a job she didn't know she was asking for. And what really pissed her off was that she was good at reading between the lines. He wanted to know if she was dirty. How far she'd go and if she could be bought. He was lucky she didn't take that music box and shove it up his ass.

"Let me make this easy for you because you don't seem too bright," Mia said. "I'm guessing you're working with the local task force, and I hope to God this is the first and only job they've ever sent you on because you're the worst operative I've ever seen. And believe me, I've see some bad ones."

Barnes stiffened. "Hey—"

"I'm not finished. You're either here for one of two reasons," she said. "You're trying to set me up and get me to agree to buy stolen goods, which seems pretty stupid considering I know there are a lot bigger fish to fry in this neck of the woods."

"I'm getting pretty tired of you calling me stupid," he said between gritted teeth.

She ignored him. "The second option is you're trying to see if you can use me for something for your own gain. You need my expertise or maybe even my shop for a setup. You're wasting your time and mine. If you'd wanted my help all you would've had to do is ask. I like cops—with the exception of you. I run a clean place with clean merchandise. I enter all my inventory into LEADS just like everyone else."

LEADS was a database where pawnshop owners entered the pieces people sold them. The first place cops looked if there were stolen items was in the LEADS database. "And I don't know what you're fishing for, but you're not going to find it here. Don't let the door hit you on the way out."

Mia moved back to the items she'd been cataloguing, but it was impossible to focus.

He tried smiling and lifting his hands like he was innocent. "Maybe we got off on the wrong foot, but you got it all wrong. I ain't no cop, and I don't know what you're talking about as far as working out any deals. I just thought we could do each other a favor or two."

"Don't they have you on a leash? I would've thought for sure one of the big dogs would've come to rescue you already. You're drowning."

His eyes narrowed to hard, mean slits, and she realized maybe he was a little older than she'd originally thought. But she hadn't been wrong about his personality. A hothead. And he was about ready to explode.

"You're a real bitch, you know that?"

"You don't say?" she said, wide-eyed. "I've never heard that before." Mia watched as he tossed the music box back into the cardboard box. She tried to even her temper and she took a couple deep breaths.

"Listen," she said, calmer. "I don't know who your commanding officer is, but let me give you some advice. I spotted you as a cop the second you got out of your truck. Go back to patrol. Undercover work is going to get you killed. You're terrible at it, Walker Barnes."

He gave her a middle finger and said, "Fuck off."

"I'm all full of fuck offs for the day, but thanks for caring. I'm a pain in the ass. I'm sure your recon on me and this shop told you that up front. Unless you didn't bother to do recon and came in blind on your superior's say-so. And if that's the case, I'm going to call you stupid again."

He grabbed her wrist and squeezed, his anger calling the shots now instead of common sense. Bingo. She knew that temper was going to get him. Now maybe she could find out what the hell he really wanted.

"I said I'm tired of you calling me stupid."

"You're going to want to let me go. Right now."

"You think you're so smart? I got news for you. You're going to help us whether you want to or not. Or we'll make sure this cesspool you love so much belongs to the government by the time we're done."

"Have you ever heard the saying, *Don't Write A Check That Your Mouth Can't Cash?*" she asked sweetly. Then she brought her free hand up and hit him under the chin with the back of her wrist. His teeth snapped together and his head jerked back. She grabbed him by the hair and slammed his face against the counter. And then she leaned over and whispered in his ear.

"Fuck you and everything you don't stand for, Walker Barnes. Or whatever your name is. You're a disgrace to the uniform and the badge, and I'm saying this here and now where everyone who's listening in can hear me. You can take your empty threats and shove them straight up your ass."

She saw a black Bronco skid to a stop in the parking lot out of the corner of her eye. Mia wasn't about to be intimidated by anyone. And she knew Sheriff MacKenzie wouldn't allow it either, even if it meant he'd have to go against another cop. Cooper MacKenzie was the real deal. And he'd always do what was right. Mia wasn't without connections of her own. She'd been a cop for ten years.

The buzzer at the door rang over and over again, and she let go of Barnes's hair so he could stand up straight. He stumbled back and looked confused. She released the switch to allow entry and slowed her breathing so the red haze of anger could fade.

The door opened and boots scraped across the hardwood floor. Something in the atmosphere changed—an electric current that was all too familiar. It heated her from the inside out, but chills pebbled across her skin. Her nipples spiked right along with her temper. It had always been that way.

Zeke McBride looked better than she remembered—though he was harder and had more of an edge. He'd always kept his dark hair shaved close to the scalp, but she could see the threads of silver sneaking in, especially around the temples. He'd always had facial hair for as long as she'd known him, but he'd let it grow to full scruff, and there was plenty of silver in that too. The age looked good on him.

His eyes were a dark forest green with flecks of gold, and he had impossibly long lashes for a man. She'd always been jealous. Those eyes never missed anything. One of his eyebrows had a scar running through it. That was new since she'd seen him last.

Zeke had always been big—several inches over six feet and muscled like a bodybuilder. The sleeves of his black shirt fit tight around his tattooed biceps and he wore jeans and a pair of steel-toed black boots. He was one-hundred percent badass, and if she still wasn't so mad at him she'd have pounced and claimed what was hers.

He'd always loved the undercover life. In his mind it was the ultimate battle of good versus evil. It was a way to feed the adrenaline rush, play within the shades of gray, and ultimately put away the bad guys.

Memories assaulted her—love and fear and chaos and danger and arguments—lots of arguments—and she was suddenly back in the place she'd been seven years before. Hurt and scared and not willing to sacrifice anything more than she already had. And he hadn't been willing to sacrifice anything at all. Or it least it had seemed that way to her. But she'd been unbending—they both had—so she'd walked away.

"Well, fuck," she said.

"It's good to see you too, Mia."

Chapter Two

Zeke McBride was a gambling man. As any self-respecting, second generation, Irish-American should be.

He'd dealt his own hand. And maybe he'd dealt from the bottom of the deck, but sometimes a man had to go to extremes when the stakes were high. And when it came to Mia, the stakes were as high as it got.

He'd used agency resources, his men, and had made damned sure their mission territory had included Surrender, Montana. He was the commanding officer of a DEA taskforce, and no one questioned the orders he gave. They'd been stuck in the middle of nowhere for three years, building covers and gaining trust within different drug running communities. They were the good guys, but sometimes the lines blurred. They were a law unto themselves, forgotten by their brothers in blue who clocked in with regular shift work—unless someone got killed.

It was Zeke's job to make sure the men remembered that there was a law and not to blur it too much. And it was his job to make sure everyone under his watch stayed alive.

His men would laugh like loons if they knew part of the reason for this mission was because of a woman. They'd call him pussy-whipped and any other names they could think of as they rolled their eyes. And then he'd have to knock some heads together just out of principal. Which was why his men were never going to find out.

Sometimes situations were so complicated and pasts so entwined that it was hard to know where to begin to start separating the threads. And honestly, this was the only thing he could come up with.

But he hadn't been prepared for the jolt that had hit him square in the chest the second he saw her again. She'd occupied his dreams for almost seven years. He'd tried dating other women—Mia was the one who'd left him after all—but he found himself searching for women that reminded him of her. The only problem was Mia had always been unique. There was *no one* like her.

Her appearance had changed, but by the steely look in her eyes, her temper had stayed very much the same. That temper had been making him go rock hard since the moment he'd met her. She could no longer pass for the role of the high school kid she'd played when she'd worked undercover. She was all woman, and a slow scan of her body did nothing to help relieve the throbbing pressure behind his zipper.

She'd always been petite, topping just a couple inches over five feet. Her Italian heritage was strong, with clear olive skin and dark eyes fringed with thick lashes that reminded him of a gypsy that could bewitch with just a look. Her brows were thick and delicately arched, and she had a mane of dark hair that made him long to feel it across his skin once more.

Her hair was longer than it had been the last time he'd seen her. And gone were the waves that had been the bane of her existence. It was thick and straight, and streaks of royal purple peaked between the black. He liked it. A lot. And high on his priority list was getting his hands in it.

She wore a plain black tank top. Her arm was covered from shoulder to wrist with an intricate sleeve tattoo, and he could see she'd added to it since the last time he'd seen her. That arm told an entire story, and he wondered if she'd added him anywhere, or if he'd even mattered enough.

Her breasts were full and filled out the tank nicely. In

fact, she'd filled out everywhere nicely. Gone was the girlish figure she'd had for most of her twenties. The way her ass filled out those jeans made his mouth water, and he remembered what it felt like to cup each round globe in his hands.

"Well, fuck," she said.

Her words pulled him back to the present. "It's good to see you too, Mia." His voice was husky and he cleared his throat. "I thought you told me you were getting as far away from this hell as you could? Looks like you didn't make it very far."

She smiled and a lesser man would've felt his balls shrivel. "No," she said politely. "I told you I was getting as far away from *you* as I could and to rot in hell."

He shrugged, unoffended. "An easy mix-up to make." He matched her smile with one of his own, and for the first time in too long he felt the embers of excitement starting to flame into anticipation.

That was the danger with working undercover. He'd been doing it for fifteen years. The fear wasn't as strong as it had once been. He had to pay closer attention to the little signs and signals that his gut used to be better at picking up on. He'd known for a couple of years it was time to get out of the game. Before he ended up getting killed or getting one of his men killed. It had taken him forty years on earth to understand what was really important in life. And she was standing right in front of him. Now he just had to prove it to her. And it looked like it was going to be a hell of a job.

Zeke looked at "Walker Barnes" and debated whether or not to rearrange his face for putting his hands on Mia. Or for just being an asshole in general. Whether he put a fist in his face or not, he could make the guy's life miserable.

"Take it back to headquarters, Baldwin. We'll talk when I get back. You're on unpaid leave until I can figure out what to do with you."

"What the hell? She just fucking tried to break my jaw."

"Every word she said is true. You pushed your way in here using intimidation and just being a dick. Your orders were simple. You're the one who chose to take them in a different direction. I didn't want you on my team to begin with, but didn't figure you'd be this stupid if I actually let you out in public. You're a disgrace to every cop that puts his life on the line. So you've got about three seconds before I don't ask you to go so nicely," Zeke said. "And if you ever touch her again you'll get to see what it's like to be someone's bitch behind bars."

Zeke almost wished Baldwin would do something stupid. He could see it in the other man's face. He had a quick temper, he wasn't a team player, and Zeke had never trusted him. He didn't deserve to carry a badge, but sometimes it was better to keep those people close where you could keep an eye on them. But Baldwin had lived out his usefulness and it was time for him to go.

The other man shifted his feet so he was in a fighting stance, and Zeke just grinned. Maybe he'd get to punch the son of a bitch after all.

"Baldwin," Mia said, before tempers could ignite any more than they already had. "Take my advice and don't be stupid. Have you ever seen Zeke fight? One punch and your skinny ass will be out cold. Leave with all your teeth intact and some of your dignity."

"Fuck you," Baldwin said. "What makes a pawnshop cunt a cop expert? Unless you just fuck so many your pussy's got radar."

"This pussy would tear you to shreds, little boy. I'm supreme cop bitch." She took a step closer and looked Baldwin up and down from head to toe. "Let me guess. You're a couple years out of the academy. Big city cop. But you're impatient. Wanted the brass without the years or the work. Why does a big city cop run away with his tail tucked between his legs and end up in Nowhere, Montana?"

Zeke was guessing Baldwin was too shocked by her accurate rundown to answer.

"I might not be working the streets anymore," she said, all serious now, "but some things never leave you. You'll never be half the cop I was or that your commander is. And if you ever touch me again you won't have to worry about being someone's bitch in prison. You'll be someone's bitch in hell. *Capisce?*"

Baldwin stared at her about two seconds before turning and walking out of the shop. He never made eye contact with Zeke. The chicken shit.

"Christ, no one gives better parting lines than you," he said, shaking his head. "You always had a mouth on you. And it always got you into trouble."

"And always got you out of trouble, if I remember right. What the hell are you doing here, Zeke? And what do you want from me?"

It was a hell of a question. One that didn't necessarily have just one answer. He made a decision and hoped it was the right one. They could deal with the other later.

"You want to know why I came here?" he asked.

Her eyes widened as he moved in and his hands went to the denim at her hips as he pushed her back against the counter. The pulse in her neck fluttered and he wanted to sink his teeth there. He wanted to sink into her every way he could.

His lips stopped a hairsbreadth from her own and he could feel the warmth of her breath. "You can give me another one of those famous parting lines later," he said. "But I'm going to do this first."

"This is a mistake, Zeke," she whispered. Her lips parted and her hands came up to grasp at his shoulders.

He whispered back, "Shut up and kiss me, Mia."

His lips covered hers—slanted over them, parted and invaded them. It was like coming home, and his body, mind, and soul recognized her as his. She'd *always* been his. Then the kiss turned from remembering and sweetness into something a little darker—a little edgier. It became more forceful, and he groaned as he felt the nip of her teeth against his bottom lip. She'd always been his match. In bed and out.

Within seconds he was lifting her by the hips so her ass rested against the counter. Her legs wrapped around his waist, and even through the denim he could feel the heat of her and knew she'd be soaking wet and ready to take him. His cock was past the point of hard and he rocked against her, drinking in her mewling cries of pleasure.

And then he did what he'd been wanting to since the minute he walked through her door. He grabbed the length of her hair and twisted it around his hand. He pulled her head back and she gasped in excitement as her throat was exposed to him. She'd always loved having her hair pulled.

"God. This is such a bad idea. Pull it harder."

He grinned and his mouth roamed just below her ear. And then he did as she asked. She was a demanding woman. And damned if he wasn't always happy to give her what she asked for.

"It's better than I remember," he said against the flesh of her neck. "Hotter—wilder."

"We never had issues in this area," she panted.

"How about we take a trip down memory lane?" He pressed against her and he thought she might orgasm just from that small touch. Her nails bit into his shoulders and he looked around quickly, trying to decide where to take her. He finally decided right where they were on the counter was good enough for him. To hell with customers or the fact that it was broad daylight. They were both so close it wouldn't last more than a few seconds anyway.

His hand went to the button of her jeans just as the buzzer rang. He swore and dropped his head down on her shoulder, his breath heaving in his chest. It took her a few seconds to realize why he'd stopped, and he smiled at the dazed look on her face. The buzzer rang again and she nudged at his shoulder for him to move back. He was surprised to find his legs weren't quite as steady as they should've been.

"It's probably for the best," she said, moving back behind the counter and pulling her hair over her shoulder so the red marks on her neck didn't show. "Eventually we'd have to get out of bed and talk. And I know that's never been one of your favorite things."

"That's where you're wrong, Mia. I've got a whole lot to talk about. We can fuck and talk as much as you'd like. Seven years is long enough to run."

She looked at him somberly and Zeke felt something go cold in his chest. "Like you said earlier, I never ran very far. Which is why I asked what you're doing here. Because if you'd really wanted me you'd have found me a long time ago."

He wanted to argue with her. To say all the things he'd said over and over again in his mind since the last time they'd seen each other. But it wasn't the time.

"I've always wanted you," he said, gruffly. "But I've got my pride too. Maybe too much of it. You said you couldn't stay and watch me die. Well guess what, sweetheart, it's seven years later and I'm still here. Look at all the time you wasted."

He turned to walk to the exit but she stopped him. "Don't forget your music box," she said. "I'm assuming you'll eventually tell me why you're really here and why Barnes wanted the authentic piece so badly."

"Maybe he was just laying it on thick."

"Nope, that part he was genuine about. Never let that kid play poker. He's got so many tells I could've filled up a book. It's a good fake, by the way."

Zeke sighed knowingly and took the box. The buzzer rang again. "Riley MacKenzie's wife works at the museum. She has a contact that can recreate certain pieces."

"Handy. Now if I only knew why you need the piece so much and why you think it's going to show up at my shop."

The corner of his lip curled up in a smile and he changed the subject. "I should probably mention that Cooper MacKenzie has loaned me the use of the apartment above the Sheriff's Office while we're working this case."

"It's nice to have friends in high places," she said. "But it's good to know you've proved my point."

"What point is that?"

Her gaze went back to his and he saw so many things

there—hurt, confusion, anger. "You didn't come here for me. You've always been incredible at undercover work. I'm a job just like any other. It's all you know. All you've ever known. Don't forget that I'm the one person who can see past the man you pretend to be. "

"Not this time. I'm not the man I used to be."

"You look the same to me. Same deceptions. Same games. Same techniques when it comes to getting me in bed. If you're that hard up for sex just say so. No need for the lies. I can be accommodating. It's been a while for me too."

"I'm not finished with you, Mia. Not by a long shot."

Mia hit the buzzer and two little old ladies shuffled through the door with a large box. Zeke passed them on the way out and reminded himself that sometimes things had to get worse before they could get better.

Chapter Three

Mia waited until dark to close the shop and head home. And she wasn't afraid to admit it was out of sheer cowardice just to stay out of Zeke's path a little longer. She needed the time to think. To try and remember all the things they'd fought about. To bring back that feeling of why she'd left to begin with. But all she could remember was how much she'd missed him. And how much she'd loved him.

She'd had nonstop customers from the moment Zeke had left, and she hadn't gotten the opportunity to take a closer look at the music box. There had to be some reason both bikers and cops would be looking for it. And no one was telling the truth. So she'd wrapped it with packing material and put it in her backpack. She had less chance of being interrupted at home.

The moon was only a sliver in the sky and heavy clouds blocked the minimal light it gave. The wind cut through her thin jacket the moment she stepped out the back door and locked up, and she realized fall was coming to a close and winter was right behind it. It was pitch black and there were no sounds or car lights from the road. There were hardly any travelers along her stretch of road after dark anyway. It had never bothered her before. But tonight her senses were tingling.

She carried her weapon down at her side and her backpack slung over her shoulder as she unlocked her 4x4 and got inside. Thoughts of the biker coming back with his brothers had never left her mind, and she sure as hell didn't want to face them unarmed. Though in reality she'd be better off using the gun on herself rather than being passed between them.

The drive into Surrender was quick and easy. The town was locked up tight for the most part. All the shops downtown were dark except for the gaslights that flickered along the walkways. There were lights coming from some of the apartments above the shops, including hers, but it looked like most of the action was happening down at Duffey's Pub at the far end of Main Street.

She rolled her window down and could hear the beat of the music from the live band. Cars littered the parking lot and every light imaginable was on, inside and out. Duffey's wasn't her scene, but still she was tempted to take a detour and head that direction. Drink a couple of beers, dance with a couple of ranch hands, and keep her mind off Zeke.

But instead, she pulled into her parking space behind the building and climbed the stairs to the second floor. If she could get a cold beer and a shower then all would be right with the world. The only issue was the man sitting in her rocking chair.

"I didn't figure you'd want me going inside without you," he said, his smile easy. As if nothing more than a simple conversation had passed between them earlier. It was one of the things that had always driven her crazy about him. When he was over something, he was over it, and he moved on. Her emotions weren't quite as settled.

"You figured right," she said. "I would've shot first and asked questions later."

"I thought that temper of yours would've settled over the years."

"Nope, I'm mean as a snake."

"That's not what the ladies at the bakery downstairs said. Those are amazing cinnamon rolls, by the way."

"I know. Why are you here again? I figure if I keep asking you'll eventually tell me."

"Don't you want to know what the ladies had to say about you?"

If she stood there looking at him too much longer she'd end up straddling his lap and throwing caution to the wind. He sent her body into overdrive—it didn't matter that it had been seven years. Hell, when they'd been together it hadn't mattered if he'd just taken her and she was still lying limp and sweaty beneath him. He always made her want him.

He lounged back in the chair like a big jungle cat, and his eyes were predatory. If she let him inside she knew where they'd end up. Even from where she stood she could feel the arcs of electricity between them. Her nipples were hard and her skin tingled. And the rigid length of his cock was visible beneath his jeans. He wasn't the least embarrassed to let her take her fill. He was a beautiful specimen of the male species. And he knew it.

"What do you say, sweetheart? Are you going to invite me in or do you want to stay out here for everyone to see? Unless you want to try that again."

Her body flushed hot and she remembered very clearly a time when they'd been on a balcony in a hotel in Mexico. The sun was brutal and small beads of sweat snaked down the hollow between her breasts, but the cool, salty breeze tickled her skin and pebbled her flesh. Waves crashed onto shore and then ebbed back in a hypnotic dance, and couples lay out on the sand in languid splendor.

And all the while, she'd been holding on to the balcony for dear life while Zeke fucked her from behind, the triangles of her bikini top pulled to the sides so her breasts were plumped and exposed. He hadn't even bothered to remove her bathing suit bottom. He'd just pushed it aside and buried himself deep.

She'd been mesmerized by all the people below. They were so close, and she'd been standing three stories above them, biting her bottom lip to keep from crying out and calling attention to herself. If they'd only looked up they'd have seen what he was doing to her, and it was that fear of getting caught that had pushed her to new limits. It had been one of the biggest rushes—the biggest turn-ons she'd ever experienced. And Zeke had held his hand over her mouth as she'd screamed through one of the most powerful orgasms she'd ever had.

Heat flushed her face as she saw the echoes of memory in his own eyes. "Come on in," she finally said, her voice husky.

She unlocked the door and went inside, leaving it open behind her. She heard the door close and the click of the deadbolt as he turned it.

"You didn't answer my question," he said.

"Well, you haven't answered any of mine." She shrugged and tossed her keys in the little bowl on the table and sat her backpack on the floor. The music box was a fleeting thought. There was no point trying to do anything with it while Zeke was there.

"Cooper and I spent the afternoon catching up over cinnamon rolls and coffee."

"I didn't realize you and Cooper knew each other that well. I just met him when I moved here."

Zeke's grin was easy to interpret. "You could say Coop and I spent some very memorable summers here when we were in college. The people in this town are still as curious as they were back then. They all remembered me. And then they started talking about you. Don't you want to know what they had to say?"

"Not really."

"I don't believe you. You're nosy as hell. I bet you know everything about each and every one of the people who work in these shops."

"Of course I do," she said over her shoulder. "Because I listen. You should try it some time."

"I've heard everything you've said since I laid eyes on you again a few hours ago."

"Yet here you are in my apartment, not answering my questions."

He grinned unrepentantly. "Listening and obeying are two different things. I'll show you the difference as soon as I get your clothes off."

She arched a brow. "Cocky bastard."

"Don't pretend you don't know where this is going, Mia. If we hadn't been interrupted today I'd have already felt that sweet pussy around me and had you screaming. And then I'd have done it again. And probably again, just for good measure."

"I find it hard to believe that you needed sex so bad you had to come all this way to get it."

"I need sex with you that bad. I've given you your space. It's time to stop running."

"I've been right here for seven years. Where have you been?" She took off her hip holster and hung it on the wall next to her bedroom door. "Oh, right. The job was more important than we were. I remember now."

"We were a team, Mia. We'd still be a team if you hadn't left. We could've had both."

"You're the only one that wanted both. I just wanted you. I guess I'm just different from you, Zeke. The body and mind can only withstand so much torture, and I watched enough friends die to last a lifetime. There comes a time when you have to evaluate your priorities and decide what's really important. What we had—what we could've had—was never important enough to you. I'm going to take a shower. You can stay or leave. It's your choice."

Mia went into her bedroom and peeled out of the jeans and tank she'd worked in all day. She'd loved being a cop. But watching her best friend executed in front of her eyes had been the last straw. It was part of the job—putting your life on the line every day—but knowing it could happen and seeing it happen were two very different things.

She'd carved out a good life for herself. It had been a risk taking her entire pension and putting it into *Pawn to Queen*. But she'd made it work, and she'd been turning a nice profit for several years. Her life as a cop was in the past. She'd left everything behind to start a new life where the nightmares weren't constantly screaming in her head. Zeke was part of that past, and she had no desire to make it her future. The lie wasn't sitting as easily as it once had.

What she needed was a shower, some hot and sweaty sex, and a good night's sleep. She just needed a little more time to prepare mentally. Zeke had been the love of her life. And she'd worked very hard over the last seven years to cauterize that wound in her heart. He wouldn't stay. He couldn't. Too many lives and operations depended on him. So all she had to do was enjoy the ride and keep her heart out of it.

"To hell with it," she said, shaking her head. She never used to be so indecisive.

Her bedroom was white. White walls, white furniture, white rug, and white bedspread. But she'd added color with bold paintings on the walls—pieces she'd loved enough that she'd decided not to sell in the shop. Gem-hued pillows sat on the bed, varied in size and shape, and the throw across the chair in the corner was emerald green. She liked pretty things. Had learned to appreciate them, as well as having the personal satisfaction of being able to choose each piece because she'd worked hard.

She grabbed a pair of thin, gray drawstring pants from the drawer and a loose black long-sleeve T-shirt, and then went into the bathroom and locked the door behind her. Not that a lock would keep him out, but she wasn't going to make it easy for him.

She found herself lingering beneath the hot spray, the scent of lemons from the soap she used permeating the air. And it wasn't long before she realized she wasn't stalling and giving herself the extra time to think. She'd already made up her mind. She was waiting for him to join her—to slip in behind her—his hands slicking over her skin and cupping her breasts and his cock pressing against her back.

Her senses were heightened, her clit throbbing and her pulse pounding. She was tempted to slide her fingers down between the folds of her sex just to take the edge off. She listened for the click of the lock on the door, but he never came.

By the time she turned the water off, the anticipation had turned into disappointment and her body thrummed with sexual frustration.

Mia toweled off quickly and put on her clothes. She knew what he was doing. She expected him to come corner her in the shower—to move things to the next level and assert his dominance—and so he did the opposite and stayed back on purpose. Just to drive her crazy. Their life had been one constant chess game of the mind after the other. It was exhilarating and exhausting all at the same time. It wasn't often a person found that kind of challenge in someone they loved.

When she came out of the bedroom she was even more surprised to find him stretched out on her sofa, his eyes closed and his breathing even.

"I'm not asleep," he said.

"Whatever you say. Are you going to tell me why you're really here?"

"Fucking you isn't a good enough reason?" he asked, arching an eyebrow.

"It's a byproduct. You wouldn't have come all this way just for that. It's a waste of work hours and manpower. You want something else too."

"If I tell you will you feed me dinner?" he asked.

"No."

"It's been a while since we've had a date," he said, ignoring her refusal.

"I don't think we ever dated. I'm pretty sure we fell into bed and then went from there."

"An oversight on both our parts. We should have a date."

"Seven years too late. But I can put a frozen pizza in the oven. Mrs. Baker downstairs gives me things to put in the freezer because she's afraid I'll starve."

"If she made it, I'll eat it," he said.

Mia kept her hands busy by putting the pizza in the oven and grabbing two bottles of beer from the fridge. She tossed him one and he snatched it out of the air with a quick flick of his wrist.

He unscrewed the bottle top and took a long pull, and then surprised her by saying, "They love you, by the way," and then he shrugged. "I know you're curious."

"No, I'm not. You just want to tell me what they had to say because cops gossip as much as the women downstairs."

"What I want is for you to stop arguing with me, you hardheaded woman. Christ knows why I find that such a turn-on."

"You always were a perverse creature."

"You'd know better than anyone. Do you have a beer to go with the pizza?"

They'd been so much more than lovers. They'd been partners. And when you combined both of those things, there were no words to describe that kind of bond. The saying of being someone's other half was true. You had to know every part of their personality—their quirks and habits—their sorrows and joy. Partners were often closer than spouses ever could be. And then when you added the sex on top of that level of personal intimacy, it was as if you didn't belong to yourself anymore.

They'd had that, once upon a time. And then she'd severed the connection like she would a limb from the body. To protect herself. He'd refused to meet her halfway. She hadn't been able to face undercover work again. Not after what had happened. And he hadn't been able to leave it behind. The job had always come first.

"Mrs. Baker said that she likes that you slip her cat treats when you think no one is looking. And there was another lady in there, she looked a little bit like a female Milton Berle—"

"That's Ginny Goodwin," Mia said, knowing exactly who he was talking about from the description.

"Well, she said that sometimes you secretly pick up the check for people over at the diner. Especially the older folks that live on social security."

"So what?" she said, feeling uncomfortable all of a sudden.

"Don't get defensive. You've made your mark here. The way you work too hard and need to take better care of yourself. Their words, not mine," he said, holding up his hands when she started to snarl. "The way you pitch in on city cleanup days or sneak into the back pew at church on Sunday mornings."

"You've got a problem with church now?"

"I don't have a problem with anything. Other than you being a big phony. Mean as a snake, my ass," he said with a grin. "You've made a home here. Become part of the community. They don't see you as an outsider. You're one of them. And one of the older ladies said she was thinking about getting some tattoos like yours and some colored streaks in her hair. She said you looked hot and she could use a little hot in her life."

Mia snorted out a laugh. The timer dinged on the oven and she pulled out Mrs. Baker's pizza. It smelled so good she had the fleeting thought that it might be best to eat it all herself.

"It'll go straight to your hips," Zeke said.

"Stay out of my head."

"Didn't have to go in there for that one. I could read the intent on your face."

He got plates and found the pizza cutter in the drawer next to the stove. She narrowed her eyes and wondered if he'd come in and looked around while she'd been hiding at work, or if her patterns of where she kept things were so regimented that he knew right where to look.

They sat at the little bar in the kitchen and ate pizza and drank beer, and Mia decided to wait him out. Zeke had never liked silence between them. He'd start talking eventually.

"I know what you're doing," he said.

She stared at him blankly and took another bite of pizza.

He finally sighed and said, "I'm retiring from undercover work."

None of the scenarios Mia had played through her mind had been that one, and she choked on her beer. She pounded at her chest and coughed a couple of times and then stared at him in complete and utter shock.

"Your mouth is hanging open," he said.

"I think I passed out for a second. I'm sorry, what did you say?"

"I should've done it years ago," he said and shrugged, ignoring her question. "I'm forty years old and it's a younger man's game. But I think sometimes it just takes men longer to realize when they've hit their limits. Our egos are fragile, I'm told."

"Are you sick or something?" she asked, only half joking. She got up and went to grab another beer. The news was a shock. And she was surprised by the violent rearing of her temper. She wanted to throw something. To ask what was so important now that he was able to put the work behind him. But she didn't. She took a long sip of beer and waited him out.

"I'm not sick. It's just time. I was offered the chief's job over in Carson. Normal hours and weekends off sounds better and better the older I get. It'd be nice to see what it's like to have a normal life."

"Wow—Carson." She still couldn't wrap her brain around it. It was like he was speaking another language and she wasn't able to process any of his words. It was a good job. Carson was the closest large city and he'd be running a full department of hundreds, not a twenty- or thirty-man task force.

"You're angry," he said, surprised.

"Nope," she denied. "Just trying to process."

"I thought you'd be happy. I thought it's what you wanted."

She debated on whether or not to throw the bottle at his head, but decided it'd be a perfectly good waste of beer. "It's what I wanted. *Past* tense. You are un-fucking-believable. What kind of ego does a man have to have to think that a woman would be waiting on him for seven years while he sowed his oats and finished up his career? And then what, Zeke? Did you think I'd run into your arms and everything would be okay?"

His cheeks flushed as his own temper rose and satisfaction crept comfortably through her.

"What makes you think that I'm not completely happy in my life as it is right now?" she asked. "Or that you'd assume I'm not involved with someone who does know the meaning of the word compromise."

"That's fucking bullshit, Mia," he said, scraping back his chair as he stood. "You gave me an ultimatum. And when I didn't cave like a whipped puppy you walked away like a spoiled brat."

"The only thing I ever asked of you was for you to love me enough. To put us first before the job for once. It was about priorities. You think I wanted to see you executed like I saw The Vaqueros do to Rachel?"

The Vaqueros were an outlaw motorcycle gang that spread from Montana and North Dakota up into parts of Canada. They ran drugs and guns and they were very good at what they did. They were one of the most violent gangs in the country.

"To stare into your eyes and see the knowledge that you were going to die just before they pulled the trigger?" she yelled. "You know as well as I do that if we hadn't busted them and caught the dirty cop giving away our identities and locations that you would be dead. Because they already had you in their sights."

"But we did catch them and we did bring them down. At least that cell. And you gave away your own identity by taking a bullet for me. Which still pisses me off."

"Because I blew my cover or because I loved you enough to try and protect you?"

"Because you almost fucking died, Mia."

"Everything that happened in that warehouse that day was a sign telling us it was time to get out. Your cover was blown, my cover was blown, and we lost three good cops. But what the hell do you do?" She was yelling and she didn't care. "You made sure yours was the first face I saw when I woke up. I was finally able to fight my way through the pain meds, and it felt like cinder blocks were sitting on top of my chest. Every breath felt like knives were stabbing me.

"And the first thing out of your mouth is that you've created a new identity and regrouped the task force to go after another Vaquero cell in a different territory. You were pissed you were going to have to lay low for a while and reestablish a new cover.

"Not once did you ever mention our relationship or that you loved me or even the fact that you were glad I was alive. All you could talk about was getting back to the job. And all I wanted was to get as far away from undercover work as I could."

She held the beer bottle to her cheek. The cool glass felt good against her heated skin. "Rachel was dead, and I felt like I should've been. Do you know how much therapy and how many years of nightmares I went through before I stopped seeing her die in my head? I needed out. That was the last straw. I couldn't function and I couldn't be a good cop. What I needed was you."

"Six weeks, Mia. Six weeks was how long it took for you to open your eyes and look at me. I was there every goddamned day and night with you. I lived and breathed you. For six weeks I'd had time to process and reassess and make decisions. I'd already said the things you wanted to hear. I begged and pleaded with you to wake up. Said prayers I hadn't remembered I'd known that you'd survive. I told you every chance I got that I loved you. But you didn't hear because your stubborn ass jumped in front of a bullet."

"And I would do it again. That bullet would've killed you. I needed you," she said again.

"And I needed to get back out there and wreak vengeance on the ones we didn't get for putting you in that hospital bed. What I needed was for you to understand."

She sighed, defeated. "There's no point in this, Zeke. The past is the past, and maybe we were just never meant to be. It was incredible while it lasted. But you and I both know cops don't make good life partners."

Mia tossed her beer bottle in the trash and moved to clear the dishes.

"I think that's bullshit. We know plenty of cops that have been able to make it work. But maybe we were both too selfish to realize what we had and how hard we had to fight for it. Maybe you're standing there now, scared to death, because you realize you didn't move on like you wanted to. Because you still love me."

Chapter Four

"You're out of your mind," she said, the words rushing out.

Zeke knew he was pushing. And he didn't care. He moved closer, boxing her in until her back pressed against the refrigerator.

"I don't think so, baby. And it's time for both of us to stop running and face the facts. We both failed each other."

The last seven years had haunted him. The mistakes they'd both made. The angry words and demands. And when it came down to it, the biggest issue was that they were both too stubborn and had too much pride. When she'd told him she was done with undercover work and that she wanted them both to move to a different area of law enforcement since it had become too dangerous, his ego had immediately reared its head.

Somewhere deep down he knew she'd been right. That getting back in the game was something he might not come out the winner of. And that was the thing—he'd wanted to win at everything—the argument, the job—and his own stubbornness had made them both losers.

The realization of what they both had to gain just by giving in a little made the tension creep from his shoulders. His body was still on high alert—how could it not be with her standing there looking flushed and angry and fuckable?

Her face was scrubbed clean, but she had a natural

beauty that had no need of makeup. Her hair was pinned up in a messy knot and strands had come loose so it framed her face. The clothes she'd put on weren't meant to entice. Just lounge pants and a long-sleeve T-shirt, but he could see how hard her nipples were beneath the cloth and he wanted nothing more than to peel her out of the layers and rediscover her body.

"You always did have an oversized ego," she sneered.

The corner of his mouth curled up in a smile. "That's not the only thing that's oversized right now. Have I mentioned how much I love a good argument with you? How wet are you, Mia? Should I take you fast and hard so we can work out the frustration, or keep you on that edge and make you beg for it?"

Her eyes dilated and her lips parted as arousal flushed her cheeks. His head dipped down and his lips hovered just above hers, giving her the chance to protest. But her dark eyes widened and stayed steady on his, and then her hands came up and rested on his chest. He thought at first she was going to push him away, but then her fingers trailed down—slowly, slowly—until they rested just above the button of his jeans.

Bombs exploded in his head and fire rushed through his nervous system. Her touch could take him places he'd never been before, and he couldn't remember ever wanting anything as badly as he wanted Mia in that moment.

His arms circled her waist and his lips moved over hers, their tongues clashing and colliding in a familiar dance. A moan escaped her throat, and her fingers jerked at the button of his jeans. He grabbed her hands.

"Too fast, baby. I'll never make it if you touch me right now."

She tasted of beer and woman, and he drank her in like a man who'd found an oasis after being lost in the desert. He pulled her closer. He wanted to consume her, surround her, until his body was part of hers. She went to his head like a drug, and a barely leashed hunger raged inside him.

"Zeke, please. Enough waiting." Her head fell back as his teeth nipped at her neck. "I can't take it anymore."

"Oh, you're going to take it, baby," he whispered. "Over and over again."

His hands moved over her, memorizing the shape of her. From her full breasts, down to her waist, and then farther down to the flare of her hips. *His.* The claiming was unmistakable.

He untied the drawstring at her waist and let the lounge pants fall to the floor. And then his hands roamed around to her ass.

"Jesus, Mia," he groaned, feeling bare skin where he'd been expecting the lace of her panties to be. He lifted her, the hard length of his cock notching against her clit. He could feel her heat, even through the denim that separated them.

Her nails bit into his shoulders and she cried out as he pressed against her. He slid a finger down her backside, over the tight bud of her anus to the creamy folds of her pussy. And then he slid a finger inside and felt her unravel in his arms.

* * * *

Every nerve in her body was screaming for more—for him to fill her completely. But even that small touch was enough to give her some relief from the glorious pleasure that had been building inside her all day. It had been too long since she'd felt Zeke hot and hard against her.

She'd always been a sexual creature, needing release like some needed food. But she'd long since grown tired of the toys she kept in her nightstand drawer or her own fingers. There was nothing quite like the feel of a hard body pressing you into a mattress.

Heat infused her and a startled cry escaped from her lips as a small orgasm ripped through her body. Her clit was swollen and rubbed against him, and she moved her hips, hoping to draw it out. But the quick release trailed off before it had barely begun and left her wanting more.

"God, Zeke. More. I'm going to go crazy if I don't have all of you."

Her hands grasped at his shirt, pulling at it until it was over his head and tossed on the floor. She wanted to feel him flesh to flesh—the hard contour of muscles beneath her fingers. He was always so fun to touch—to look at. The shadows cast his face in a savage light, the dark scruff of his beard a contrast to his chiseled cheekbones and square jaw. He was, quite simply, beautiful.

His hands tightened on her ass and her legs wrapped like a vise around him, looking for another quick thrill before they got down to serious business. No one could command her body like he could—a maestro of touch, building crescendo after crescendo until she screamed at the pinnacle of pleasure.

He moved quickly toward the bedroom and jerked back her comforter, laying her down on the cool white sheets. He discarded her shirt and looked his fill. His finger touched the scar just above her breast and his face darkened. If that scar was just a hair to the left she wouldn't be here. And she realized it was the first time he'd seen her naked since she'd gotten it.

She felt exposed, even though he'd seen her laid out before him a thousand times before, but that thought quickly passed as his eyes darkened with desire and his breathing grew heavy. His finger trailed from the scar down to the rosy tip of her breast and she felt powerless beneath his touch. And then she remembered that she wasn't without her own brand of power.

"Mmm, you're bigger than I remember," she said, eyeing his broad chest with appreciation.

"Working out becomes an obsession when you don't have a personal life."

Her hands skimmed up her stomach slowly and his eyes followed, until she was cupping her breasts. They were full and heavy and ached with the need for his mouth. She tweaked her nipples between her thumb and forefinger and moaned as frissons of pleasure went straight to her clit.

"Christ, Mia. You'll make me come before I can get inside of you."

"Better hurry and get inside of me then," she dared.

"Witch." He loomed over her, the muscles in his arms bulging as he supported himself. And then he lowered his head and his tongue flicked a rigid nipple before taking it in his mouth completely. Her back arched as she pressed against him, her hands holding the back of his head so he'd never leave her.

He blew a cool stream of air across her nipple and she shivered in response. "I once could make you come just by touching you here," he said. "They're so sensitive. I've never seen anything like it."

"I'd rather feel you inside me," she panted as his teeth clamped down on a nipple. The sizzle rippled through her nervous system, and her clit throbbed with the pounding beat of her heart. She shivered and convulsed as he bit a little harder, just so there was a slight edge of pain, and then he suckled her, massaging her other breast at the same time. The suckling grew more intense, until she could feel each tug between her thighs. And then stars exploded behind her closed eyelids and she was crying out as wave after wave of pleasure consumed her.

She felt the bed shift and his weight lift as he discarded his jeans, but she was too relaxed to open her eyes and watch. She could've curled up like a cat and gone to sleep.

"Oh, no you don't," Zeke said.

She could hear the smile in his voice and her eyelids fluttered half open as he crawled back on the bed. And then her eyes widened and she cried out as he slid inside of her straight to the hilt. Her breath caught in her throat and her hips arched against him. She was wet, but the tissue inside her vagina was swollen from the small orgasms she'd had and his fit was more than snug.

It was like coming home after a long journey. Foreign and familiar all at once. The feel of his skin against hers, the way his chest hair abraded her nipples. She couldn't deny it. He'd always held her heart.

"God, Zeke. Love me."

She regretted the words instantly, and then had the

hopes that maybe he hadn't heard her after all. His chest rumbled and an animalistic growl escaped from his throat. His dick went impossibly hard and grew in size as he came closer and closer to his own orgasm. He continued to pummel inside her relentlessly and she held on, her mouth open in a silent scream as the head of his cock touched somewhere deep inside of her—to a place that made the world go dark and explosions detonate from her womb and spread through her limbs until the muscles went rigid and the beginnings of an intense pleasure spiraled from the inside out.

She wasn't sure she could survive it, and knew he'd branded her like he never had before. Sensations built inside her until a deep, pulsing starburst of pleasure erupted through her core, coursing through her body. Her muscles spasmed, her limbs stiffened, and she cried out his name as he called out hers. Hot jets of his semen filled her and she tightened around him, wanting to take him all.

And then there was nothing but darkness as sleep consumed her.

* * * *

Zeke had never dreamed with such clarity before. Where his senses were primed so every sound was magnified and the slightest touch could send his body soaring. He had to be dreaming because nothing outside of dreams could feel like this.

His eyelids felt weighted down and he barely had the energy to grasp at the sheets beneath him as the liquid heat of Mia's mouth clamped around his cock. Her tongue swirled around the sensitive skin of his head before swallowing him whole. And she repeated the pattern over and over until his hips arched and he was fucking her mouth in earnest. And then she stopped and pulled away, and he groaned in protest.

"It's my turn," she whispered. "You'll lie there and take it."

And then he realized maybe he wasn't dreaming after all.

He forced his eyes open and looked down the length of his body to see her between his thighs, his cock hard and sticking straight up and wet from her mouth, the veins bulging.

A small amount of light seeped in through the blinds from the porch light she'd left on. Her eyes were dark and seductive and her smile was wicked. She was in a playful mood.

"I thought I was dreaming," he said.

Her brow arched and her tongue flicked out, making his cock jerk. "Reality is always better."

"So I've discovered." He gritted his teeth as her hot little fist wrapped around the base of his cock and her tongue continued to wreak havoc on his system.

"I've always loved the way you feel. The way my mouth and tongue have learned the shape of you. Every ridge. The way you swell in my mouth just before you're going to come and the taste of you as I drink every drop."

"Jesus, Mia," he panted, his hands going to her head, his fingers tangling in her hair.

"Mmm," she moaned, swallowing him whole once more.

Her head moved up and down between his thighs and her mouth clamped tighter around him, milking him with every stroke. His balls were tight and he'd be done for in a couple more strokes if she didn't slow down.

"Enough," he begged. "I don't want to come yet." His gaze met hers as she looked up from the object of her focus. And the sight of his cock in her mouth while she stared at him out of those gypsy eyes was one of the sexiest fucking things he'd ever seen.

"Are you giving me orders?" she purred sweetly, licking him once more, like a cat, from base to tip.

"Has it ever done any good outside of an undercover op?"

"No," she said, smiling cheekily. And then she released him and sat up on her knees, steadying herself on his muscled thighs.

She looked like a goddess rising over him—powerful and

wicked and just a little bit dangerous. Dark hair fell over her shoulders, covering one of her breasts completely and leaving the other exposed. Her muscles were toned—years of discipline and exercise keeping her fit even after she left the job—and his eyes were immediately drawn to the silver bar piercing at her belly button.

"I meant to tell you earlier that I like the piercing, but I was too busy fucking you."

Her lips quirked and her hand left his thigh to skim across her stomach, tracing the bar with her finger. "Yes, you were. Now it's my turn to fuck you."

His cock jerked as she said it. He'd always loved when she talked dirty. And then he lost his train of thought as she straddled his hips and sank down all the way to the hilt. She fit him like a fucking glove and his jaw clenched and his hands went to her hips as he struggled for control. His body was an inferno and he was surprised it was physically possible to withstand that kind of heat.

Her muscles contracted around him and then she threw her head back and rode him with abandon, her hips undulating and her vaginal muscles squeezing him in perfect time. Until he thought he'd lose his mind with the pleasure.

Then he felt the liquid heat of her surround his cock, the ripple of contractions and her screams of pleasure as her orgasm ripped through her. And he was helpless to stop himself from following after her.

Chapter Five

The shrill scream of the alarm coming from her phone jerked her out of a deep sleep. Three loud raps at the door followed soon after.

"What the hell?" Zeke asked, rolling out of bed in a fluid motion and grabbing his duty weapon.

"That's the alert for my shop alarm system," she said, turning off the phone.

Mia grabbed the gun she had in her nightstand and moved in a crouched motion to the chair in the corner where a gray pair of sweats were folded. She dressed quickly, but Zeke had already pulled on his jeans and was heading to the front door.

"Wait, dammit," she hissed. "It's my house."

"It's Cooper," Zeke said. "I looked through the blinds in the bedroom." He moved to the side and let her answer the door.

"My shop?" she said to Cooper, by way of greeting.

Cooper nodded. "There's been an attempted break-in. I don't know how bad or if they breached the inside. I was just on my way into the office this morning when the alarm company called through. The deputy on duty called me and I figured it was faster to stop here first."

She could smell the soap from Cooper's morning shower

and his black hair was still damp at the tips. He was dressed for work—a chambray button down shirt with the Surrender Sheriff's Office logo embroidered over the pocket and a pair of jeans and boots. He wore a shoulder holster and his badge was pinned on the left side of his shirt.

"I'll meet you there," he said.

"Thanks, we'll be right behind you."

Mia headed back to the bedroom in a daze. She heard the mumble of Zeke and Cooper's words as they talked, but everything was buzzing in her head and all she could think about was her shop and what that small piece of land and the building that sat on it meant—it was the symbol of her new life, of her independence. And now someone had violated that. It didn't go unnoticed that the breach and the appearance of Zeke had happened all in the same twenty-four-hour time period. That was something to think about later.

She looked at the clock and hadn't realized it was just past five. It was still dark outside and the air was bitter with the chill. It wouldn't be long before the first frost hit. Clothes were easy—a pair of jeans, a sweatshirt, and her boots. She pulled her hair back in a ponytail and topped it with a baseball cap. And then she grabbed her holster from the hook she'd hung it from the night before and strapped it on.

It didn't go past her notice that she and Zeke had fallen into a familiar routine. They'd lived together for a couple of years on and off, depending on if she had to live with a family to give the illusion that she was a student. They knew where to move and which order to do things in to be the most efficient so they could get where they needed to go.

By the time she grabbed her car keys and backpack, he was holding the front door open for her. They were both cautious as they approached her 4x4, scanning the area for signs of a threat. But all was clear and she got behind the wheel. He always hated it when she drove. It was funny how those memories came back now, when she'd forgotten the little details of their relationship during their time apart.

"Anything you want to tell me before we get there?" Mia asked.

She drove down Main Street—the lights were on in the bakery and early birds were coming in for breakfast. Lights were on or flickering on in a few of the other shops, but she barely glanced at them. They were all looking at her as she drove by, however. There was no doubt the word had already started to spread about her shop. At least ten people she knew of had police scanners and kept everyone informed of any misdoings in the community.

She drove past Charlie's Automotive and then climbed the hill that led out of Surrender. Fiery fingers of the blazing morning sun crept over the landscape as she peaked the hill and then began the descent down the other side.

All in all, it wasn't a long drive. Maybe fifteen minutes. But it had felt like an eternity.

Zeke went still and quiet beside her. She recognized the blank look on his face. It was the same one he'd always had whenever he was trying to keep something from her.

"Let's just check it out and see if any damage was done," he finally said. "Maybe it was someone looking for some fast cash."

"This is my life, Zeke. Don't try to fuck me over. And don't try to feed me lines about you retiring from undercover work. All of a sudden seven years seems like an eternity. I don't know you anymore. And there's no reason to trust you."

"You have every reason to trust me. I love you, and as soon as this job is over I'm done. I just need to gather some facts before I start talking about things that might not have anything to do with you and everything to do with keeping other people alive."

Mia stayed quiet, not sure how to respond to his declaration of love. He'd never been one to say it often, but when he did she treasured those moments. And she hated that she couldn't be sure he meant it this time. Time had passed. Things had changed. And there was always an agenda.

She parked next to Cooper's Tahoe in the back of the parking lot. There was another truck she didn't recognize parked next to him, and three men stood in front of it. A fire truck with flashing lights was parked to the side of the building, but far enough away not to damage the scene. She tried not to despair at the sight of her missing front door. Other than that, on the outside, it looked untouched.

At least the building was standing. Anything else she could deal with. As if reading her mind, Zeke squeezed her shoulder as they walked over to the others, but she shrugged him off. Sympathy wasn't what she needed at that moment. Not if she wanted to keep it together. What she really needed was a cup of coffee.

"The alarm company silenced the alarms," Cooper said. "You'll need to call them to set things back up once you're ready to roll."

"Definitely not someone passing by looking for a quick buck," Zeke said, hands on hips as he surveyed the scene.

"Not by a long shot. They came prepared and knew what they were doing. Deputy Greyson was first on scene. The fire department pulled in right after him."

Mia knew Lane Greyson well. His wife, Naya, was one of her closest friends. Naya was a bounty hunter, and they'd hit it off immediately.

"Sorry about this, Mia," Lane said. "I know what this place means to you."

"Is the inside as bad as I think it's going to be?" she asked him.

His lips pinched together. "I brought you a to-go cup of coffee. It's in the cab of my truck."

"That bad, huh," she said, her stomach tied in knots. She went to the cab of the truck and opened the door, grabbing the thermal coffee mug from the middle console. Zeke introduced himself to Lane and they shook hands, and then he shook hands with Riley MacKenzie and slapped him on the shoulder. Mia was guessing he knew all the MacKenzie brothers as well as he did

Cooper.

"What dragged you out of bed before noon?" Zeke asked Riley.

Where Cooper was dark-haired and blue-eyed, Riley was his polar opposite with blond hair and brown eyes. They had the same square jaw and eye shape, but at first glance it was hard to tell they were brothers. And then she looked closer and noticed they were very much cut from the same cloth, with broad builds and fighting man's hands. Neither of them looked as if they'd ever backed away from a fight. No wonder Zeke got along so well with them. He carried himself the same way.

"A crying baby," Riley answered. "It was my shift for middle of the night duty, so I was wide awake when Cooper texted. Of course, by the time I left the house the baby was sleeping again and the whole house was quiet. I figured it'd be better to tag along than to get my hopes up by lying down and trying to go to sleep."

"Sounds like fun," Zeke said. "I'm thinking of having kids in the next forty years or so."

"Hey, Picasso did it. It's good to have goals, man."

"Has there been time to secure the scene?" Mia asked. She knew the drill. Knew they were standing out in the parking lot for a reason. But God, she wanted to get in there and see what they'd destroyed.

"We walked the perimeter when we arrived," Cooper said. "Anyone who was here was long gone, but you'll see the marks on the sidewalk. I put the word out for who we're looking for."

Mia followed them toward the front of the shop, her boots crunching over gravel. She didn't see what Cooper was talking about until she was almost on top of it.

"Skid marks," she said. And one of the motorcycles who'd left it had ridden up her stairs and left them on the porch as well.

"Any reason why a group of bikers would pay you a visit, Mia?" Zeke asked.

Unlike the rookie who'd been standing in her shop yesterday, she knew how to lie. Years of practice made it as easy as breathing. There were techniques they'd been taught at specials ops classes that helped with the art of lying—body language, facial expressions, and making sure the lies were close enough to the truth that you didn't forget and stumble somewhere along the way.

"Not that I can think of," she answered. The music box was still in her backpack in the car. She knew she'd have to tell Zeke about the biker and the music box, but now wasn't the time or the place. If the details were part of whatever op he was running then Cooper and the others wouldn't know what was going on. And anything they found out could endanger a life.

She looked at Zeke and asked, "Any coincidence as to why bikers would show up and do this the same day you roll back into my life?"

"Not that I can think of," he said, parroting her.

"We didn't find any other breached areas," Cooper said, heading up the short stairs to her porch. "They knew the entry point they wanted and knew how to enter. This is a reinforced steel door and at night you pull down the cage behind it for added security."

"Yeah, but nothing is infallible," she said. "Obviously. But it's a time-consuming job. They had to cut through the hinges and remove the door completely. The alarm would've been sounding, but guys like that wouldn't care. And they'd have the right tools on hand to be able to get in. They'd use the same blade on the pull-down cage and then walk in. There are at least eight or ten skid marks and grooves dug into the gravel of the parking lot."

"Ballsy to draw such attention to themselves," Lane said.

"No one is ever on this stretch of road after midnight."

Zeke walked off toward the road and she could tell he was trying to get a better feel for how many there were, which direction they'd entered from, and hopefully, which direction they'd exited.

"They'd know Surrender would be the closest responding department," Mia said.

"And that we only have one on-duty officer working the night shift," Cooper finished for her, his look grim. "Proof of the liabilities of being a small town and working with a limited budget."

"This isn't your fault." She wanted to make sure he knew that. "It's location and timing. I'm pretty far outside of town. By design. And even though I'm technically part of Surrender, you and I both know that if I were on the other side of that hill with the other businesses, this never would've happened. But I'm not and there's no easy way for emergency personnel to get here. They knew they had at least twenty minutes to get the job done."

Zeke walked back to their group and said, "They split off in each direction. Pretty typical behavior. We can assume this is the work of The Vaqueros since this is their territory. And they're known to converge on a location, wreak havoc, and then separate so they can lay low for a while. They're well organized and they run an intelligent operation. I've watched the way they work from the inside. It's why they've been so successful running drugs these past years. They're like ghosts."

"We can try and pull identities from the security cameras," she said, "but knowing who they are won't help us on how to find them. Identifying them and plastering their faces on the news is like a badge of honor."

"Which brings us back to the question," Riley said. "Why here and why you?"

Cooper looked at her and said, "Have you had any run-ins with The Vaqueros?"

"I threatened to shoot one yesterday," she said. "I suppose he could've taken it personally."

All four men stared at her with varying degrees of surprise on their faces. "What? You know I'm always armed and I don't put up with bullshit in my place."

"Or maybe you could've mentioned it?" Zeke said.

"When would've been a good time? When you popped

up in my shop asking for the same item the biker was, or maybe when you showed up at my apartment to get me into bed? You're right, Zeke. I should've confessed the second you showed up. My bad."

Riley coughed to cover a laugh and Cooper looked down at his boots, but she could see his smile. Lane never showed much expression at all, but she knew him well enough to see that he wanted to smile.

Zeke's jaw was clenched hard and all he said was, "Mia," in that tone of voice that didn't bode well.

She arched a brow and narrowed her eyes. Now wasn't the time for him to try any macho bullshit.

"Might as well check out the inside," Cooper said. "You can see if anything is missing."

They stepped through the gaping hole where her front door had once been, and Mia had to stifle a gasp. Her heart thudded in her chest and a red haze clouded her vision. Everything was destroyed. The shelves were knocked down, the floor littered with broken glass. They'd not gotten the more expensive pieces locked behind the counter, though she could see the scratches on the bulletproof glass.

"What was the biker looking for?" Cooper asked.

Mia stepped over glass and an electric guitar that was broken in half. "He asked for a music box. Was very specific about what kind he wanted. He said that he'd been told someone had come in and sold it to me. He offered to double my money." She could hear the hollowness of her own voice.

"I told him he was mistaken and that I didn't have a piece like that. He got close and told me I'd better rethink my answer, so I cocked the sawed off I've got stashed under the counter. He decided to leave after that."

"He make any threats?"

She sighed. "Yeah, he said he'd come back for a visit with his brothers."

"Jesus, Mia," Zeke said. "Why wouldn't you report something like that?"

"Because I can take care of myself," she said, whirling on Zeke. "I was a cop, remember? How would reporting it have changed anything? There's not enough manpower to put out a protection detail."

"And now you've got a target on your back."

"They did what they came to do," she said. "They destroyed and still didn't find what they were looking for. There's no reason for them to come back here. But they might target other pawnshops in the area if their intel tells them that's where the music box ended up."

"We'll put an alert out to all the surrounding areas," Cooper said. "We'll get in and out of here quickly so you can get the insurance company in and start going through your inventory."

"What's left of it," she said, looking around at the shambles of a room.

"I'll grab Thomas and Dane and we'll come back and put in a makeshift door with a sturdy deadbolt," Riley said, speaking of his other two brothers. "At least it'll deter anyone wanting to snoop or help themselves to what's available."

"I'd appreciate it. This is definitely going to put a dent in my new parking lot fund."

"I can call in a couple of favors," Zeke said. "I've got men at the DEA office that are twiddling their thumbs, waiting for a big case to drop. They can set up a patrol in the area and keep an eye out to make sure you don't get another visit."

"We'll coordinate with the surrounding departments and set up checkpoints and hot spots. The problem with The Vaqueros is their clubhouses are in the mountains. We might not see them for weeks. Or until they need supplies. And if we get a snowfall during that time it could be even longer."

"Lovely," Mia said. "Well, there's no use wasting time when there's work to be done. How soon do you think I can call insurance and we can start cleanup?"

"Should be ready for insurance this evening if he's available. You can probably start cleanup tomorrow."

She nodded and glanced at Zeke. He was staring at a painting that had fallen off the wall like it held the secret of life. It was a contemporary oil with bright colors, and she'd briefly thought about taking it home and hanging it in her dining room.

She thought about the music box tucked safely in her bag. She needed to get rid of Zeke so she could go through it in private. He'd been too secretive since his arrival the day before, and no matter what he said about still loving her, seven years was a long time. And people changed. Especially people who'd lived that underground life and spent their days and nights lying to people. She wasn't about to get caught in the middle of something that might ruin the life she'd built for herself.

As if reading her mind, Zeke turned his head and looked at her intently. "I'm bunking with you," he said. "And don't even think about arguing. I'll sleep on the couch if I have to, but it's too dangerous. You need someone to watch your back."

Or he needed to be right in the thick of things and she was the easiest access point, she thought.

Chapter Six

A week later, the first frost glittered across the top of the ground like tiny diamonds. And to Mia's surprise and supreme gratitude, her shop was cleaned up, the door repaired, and she'd managed to restock some of her inventory.

She'd never expected the outpouring of support from the community, and she never would've thought to ask for it. But almost as soon as she'd gotten back into town people were stopping her on the street, asking what they could do to help. And then the next morning, a group of people showed up at her shop unannounced with brooms and vacuums and cleaning supplies, and they all got to work.

She still didn't know how to respond. A thank you seemed inadequate. In her line of work she'd never expected the best from people, so their generosity astounded her. People donated items they were getting rid of, so by the end of the week everything looked almost as it had before, though the shelves were still a little bare.

Zeke had been true to his word and had stayed at her place. She hated to admit it, but having him there did ease her mind a bit. She'd been annoyed at his high-handedness and had given him an extra pillow and a blanket for the couch that first night after the break-in. He'd taken it with a smirk and a wicked glint in his eyes.

And then she'd been woken up sometime in the middle of the night, her shirt pushed up around her waist and his head between her thighs. She'd been dreaming of him, and then she'd woken to find her dream a reality. He hadn't slept on the couch since, and her muscles were sore in all the right places. Zeke had always been a thorough and athletic lover.

They also hadn't spoken of the past or his work. He still hadn't told her why he'd really come. But he'd continued to say he was retiring from undercover work, to the point that she wanted to believe him. He had to give the mayor an answer about the chief's job in Carson by the end of the month, and she'd be lying if it hadn't sneaked into her mind that Carson wasn't all that far of a commute from Surrender.

She'd forgotten how comfortable they'd always been with each other—the easy conversations, the things they had in common, the sports teams they argued over. Remembering the arguments had been the easiest thing to do. But there'd been more good times than bad.

They'd fallen into an easy rhythm. He'd leave sometime after midnight and go into work, or he'd disappear for an hour or so at random times throughout the day. Then he'd show up randomly at her shop, pitch in to help, and leave again. She remembered how it was. The erratic schedules. The missed sleep, anniversaries, holidays, and birthdays. The only difference was he no longer talked to her about work. It was the albatross in the room.

"You ready to call it a night?" he asked as she looked over the shop one final time to make sure everything was in place. She'd be back open for business on Monday.

"More than ready. I need a hot bath and pizza. Maybe a pizza while sitting in the hot bath."

"How about a trip to Duffey's instead? We can play a game of pool, eat hot wings, and drink half-price beer."

"Well, hell, that sounds way better than soaking my aching feet."

He grinned and tossed an arm around her shoulder,

pulling her close. "I'll spot you a couple of balls since you're so tired."

"The hell you will," she said, her spine straightening.

He chuckled and they headed to Duffey's. It was the after-work crowd for the most part, but a lot of them had already thinned out to head home for dinner. The live music didn't start until ten o'clock, so they still had time to play and be able to hear themselves.

Duffey's didn't cater to the tourist crowd. It was a local bar with sawdust on the floors, scarred tables, and draft beer and a small selection of wine. There were no mixed drinks or cocktails. Trophy antlers hung on all the walls and she was pretty sure they'd never seen a dust rag.

Zeke went to the bar to order drinks and chatted with Duffey while he was waiting. She'd learned over the last several years that Duffey never smiled. He'd owned the bar for close to fifty years, and from the pictures hanging on the wall, he hadn't changed a bit in those fifty years. He always wore a white undershirt and trousers with a larger white butcher apron tied several times around his scrawny waist. The tuft of gray hair circling the bald patch on the top of his hair was coarse and wiry, and round, wire-framed glasses sat perched at the end of his nose. His lips were thin and he always looked like he'd just swallowed something sour.

Mia had learned early on that the best course of action was to stay off his radar, so she headed toward the back room where the pool tables were located. She passed Jana Metcalfe along the way. Jana had been a waitress at Duffey's since long before Mia had moved there. She was pleasantly plump and somewhere in her mid to late thirties, and she always had a wide and infectious smile.

"Is the pool table taken?" Mia asked her.

"A group just cleared out. It's all yours." She gathered empties from a table, balancing the tray and making it look effortless. "It's good to see Zeke back in town," she said, conversationally. "Almost didn't recognize him. He looks a lot different than he did at nineteen." She winked and chuckled. "He spent a lot of summers here. Lord, he and those MacKenzies got into some trouble. I'm surprised Duffey even lets any of them in the door."

"He must not be too mad," Mia said. "They're talking to each other."

"That's because Duffey is still trying to get Zeke to pay for some damages. Duffey just likes to complain. He'll overcharge Zeke for the beers and then he'll feel like he's gotten away with something. Let me give you a tip. When you're ready to order anything else, come find me. I'll make sure your ticket is right."

Mia shook her head and smiled. "Thanks, I appreciate it."

"Hey, you guys have had a rough week. Duffey should be giving you the beer." Jana stretched her neck out to the side to look around the corner toward Duffey. "Don't tell him I said that. That man's never given away a thing in his life."

"Why do you work for him?"

"I'm his granddaughter." Jana winked and smiled again, and then hefted the tray onto her shoulder and headed toward the kitchen.

Mia already felt the tension draining from her shoulders. Zeke had been right. It was nice to get out. They'd been cooped up at the shop or her apartment all week. It had been nothing but work and worry.

She headed to the far back of the restaurant and took the little hallway to the left. It was a private room they sometimes used for bachelor parties, but it was the only area big enough for the pool table. She tossed her leather jacket over a chair and went to check the cues. And then she racked the balls and waited for Zeke to arrive. *Spot her a couple balls her ass.*

* * * *

Zeke came in with a pitcher of beer and two frosted mugs, and it was a damned good thing he'd had a good grip on them. Mia was his every fantasy, and the sight of her leaning on her cue stick in worn jeans and a stretchy white top made his cock hard enough to drive nails. She'd let the natural curl in her hair reign free and it flowed down her back, tempting him.

The thought crossed his mind that he might be better off tossing her over his shoulder and heading back home, but then another idea came to mind. He kicked the door shut with the heel of his foot and brought the beer over to one of the little round tables, pouring them each a glass.

"Did you order dinner?" he asked.

"Not yet." She took a sip of beer and licked her lips, and he swore he felt her tongue straight down his dick. "I figured we could eat after I beat you a couple of times."

He arched a brow and grinned. "Now you're talking my language. What do you say we make it interesting."

"Irish boy," she said with a smile. "Everything's a bet."

"Life's a bet. So?" he asked. "You in?"

"What are the rules?"

"Winner takes two out of three games. Straight pool." He answered.

"And what do I get when I win?" she asked, arching a brow.

He laughed and felt the adrenaline surge through him. "Winner gets to be on top. And the loser has to do whatever the winner demands."

"Ahh, so laundry and doing the dishes. Sounds like a deal to me."

"Be careful, Mia. I haven't forgotten how to spank you."

"Mmm," she said. "You'd have to win to try it."

"Challenge accepted. Rack 'em."

Mia set her cue against the wall and went to the opposite end of the table, leaning over and pressing the balls tight in the triangular rack. Then she lifted it carefully. He could see right down the vee of her shirt to the soft mounds of her breasts and the lacy white bra that barely covered them. His cock had been hard from the second he'd imagined her stretched across that pool table, and he hoped he could concentrate enough to put his money where his mouth was. She was a temptress, and he wanted to be tempted.

As soon as the cue stick was in his hand, his competitive streak took hold. This wasn't a game he wanted to lose. He broke and the clack of balls hitting was like music to his ears. They'd spent a lot of time in pool halls over the years, watching drug deals go down or just becoming known in the community.

By the end of the second game, he was starting to worry that he might be doing laundry and dishes after all. He'd won the first game. Barely. And she'd taken the second game that had been equally as close as the first.

"You want to quit?" she asked.

"Are you forfeiting? Because if you forfeit that means I win." He waggled his eyebrows and said, "And I've been seeing my handprints on your ass in my head ever since I mentioned it."

"You're a sadistic bastard, McBride."

"You never used to complain, baby."

"Your break. Unless *you* want to forfeit. I've got a pretty amazing fantasy going through my head too. I'll let you wear my apron while you're doing the dishes."

"I'm just adding a tally of strokes that are going to show red on that sweet ass of yours. Keep talking, sweetheart. My hand is itching."

The corner of her mouth curled up in a smile and he recognized the look in her eyes. It was the look she had just before he usually found himself flat on his back with her hot mouth around his cock.

The game went quickly. He ran the table and then just missed getting the eight ball in the side pocket. He was sweating bullets as Mia had her own run of luck. She lined up her final shot, and he held his breath as she pulled back the cue stick. And then he watched in disbelief as her cue shifted just slightly out of alignment as she made the shot. The eight ball went in the corner pocket. But the cue ball didn't stop like it should have. It spun back and went in the side pocket on the opposite side of the table.

Zeke's eyes met hers as she looked up at him over her cue stick.

"Looks like I missed," she said.

"Looks like you did."

He didn't remember how he got to the other side of the table where she was standing so quickly. He only knew she was there and his mouth was on hers—hot and wet—devouring. He couldn't stop. Wouldn't stop.

His tongue caressed hers and he shuddered as her fingers curled around his shoulders, her nails biting into them.

"God, Mia. You drive me crazy." His hands skimmed down her sides and he grabbed her hips, pulling her against him so she could feel the rigid length of his cock. His teeth nipped at her lips and he drank in her gasp.

"Let's go," she panted. "I want you inside me." Her head was arched back so her neck was exposed and her eyes were half closed, her lips swollen from his kiss.

"I won, baby. My rules. My demands. I'm going to fuck you right here." He felt her shiver against him and knew the idea of being caught was always a sexual high for her.

She shook her head. "No, Zeke. We'll be caught."

"Not if you don't scream," he whispered against her ear. "I'm going to fuck you. And you're going to feel the heat of my hand against your ass."

His arm wrapped around her waist and he spun and lifted her so she sat on the edge of the pool table. There wasn't a lock on the door, and they could both hear the rumble of voices and the clank of glasses from the bar. Their time was limited, so he knew he had no choice but to give them what they both needed fast and hard. He could take his time later, once they'd gotten home.

* * * *

Mia gasped as he lifted her onto the pool table. His mouth found her lips and then his teeth nipped playfully. His mouth moved down her neck and the rasp of his beard scraped against her jaw. She arched into him and felt the hard ridge of his cock press against her clit.

He always pushed her sexually. To discover what she liked, what she feared, and what turned her on. Sometimes the discoveries intertwined.

"God, Zeke. Hurry."

His hands came up and grabbed at the vee of her T-shirt, and then he ripped it right down the middle, exposing her bra. Her nipples tightened and her eyes widened with excitement. Her heart pounded in her chest and liquid pooled between her thighs. Her clit throbbed, and she knew it would take very little to plummet her over the edge.

"You are so fucking beautiful." His voice was rough and raspy and she shivered against him. And then his fingers flicked at the front clasp of her bra and her breasts were exposed to him.

"And you're making me crazy," she panted. "I said hurry."

"Baby, you know it never does any good to give me orders. I'm contrary like that. And I won. I'm issuing the orders here."

"You won because I threw the game. I decided getting fucked sounded a hell of a lot better than watching you do my laundry."

His fingers went to the button of her jeans and flicked them open. She lifted her hips so he could pull her jeans and underwear down to her ankles. Her boots were in the way and she growled in frustration at not being able to get her legs wrapped around him.

"Let me tell you a secret," he whispered. "Even if you'd won you'd still be sitting here on this table with your jeans around your ankles and your tits exposed to the world. You're too tempting, baby."

His fingers were rough and trailed over her hip to the slick flesh of her pussy. She was swollen and sensitive, and she hissed as he rubbed against her opening, sending pleasure straight to the taut bud of her clit. She was so close to coming her body tensed and her legs shook with anticipation.

"Anyone could walk in at any time," he said, continuing to stroke her. "Do you know what they'd see?"

"Zeke," she groaned, trying to move her hips against his fingers, but he had her anchored to the pool table with his arm.

"They'd walk in and see a woman so fucking sexy they'd be seeing you in their wet dreams from now on. A body that makes a man want to sit up and beg." He squeezed the hard muscles of her bicep and then brought his hand down so it cupped her breast gently. "You're hard and soft, all at the same time." His hand trailed down farther until he cupped her pussy again. "And then they'd see this—bare and pink and wet—just waiting to be fucked."

"Why don't you put your money where your mouth is, hotshot? Or in this case, why don't you put your dick in my pussy and we'll call it even."

"Fuck, that mouth of yours, Mia. Always getting you into trouble."

"If by trouble, you mean fucked, then thank God for my mouth."

She gasped and then laughed as Zeke pulled her to a standing position, turned her around, and then pressed his hand against her back so her breasts rasped against the felt of the pool table.

Anticipation soared through her as she heard the rattle of his belt being undone and the rasp of his zipper. And then she felt the thick head of his cock push between her thighs. He teased her, rubbing his dick through her wetness, and then she felt the burning and stretching of her pussy as he slid inside of her.

"Ohmigod," she moaned, her head arching back as her breath caught. She couldn't spread her legs because of the binding around her ankles, so the fit was tighter and she felt every inch of him as he invaded her. And then he was embedded to the hilt and she felt his testicles slap against the lips of her cunt.

He pulled back slowly and she felt every stretch of tissue before he rammed home again. Her mouth opened on a silent scream as pleasure unlike anything she'd ever experienced arced through her body. Her muscles tightened around him and liquid honey coated his cock, and then he settled into a pounding rhythm that sent sensations tearing through her.

"Fuck, you're so tight. I'm not going to last long, baby. Let me feel that sweet pussy squeeze me tight while you come."

She heard the strain in his voice and felt his cock swell the closer he got to orgasm. The head of his cock pressed against her G-spot every time he thrust inside her and her fingers scraped at the felt of the table, trying to find something to anchor her during the storm that had taken over her body.

"Come on, baby. Come on," he panted.

And then she felt it. He pushed against her G-spot one more time and held there. Waves of sensation stole her breath. Her pussy clenched around him, spasming as the orgasm took her by surprise with its intensity. Her eyes rolled back in her head and she was vaguely aware that his hand clamped over her mouth as she began to scream out her release. She didn't care. A hundred people could've rushed through the door at that moment and her orgasm wouldn't have stopped. She was powerless against it—against the debilitating pleasure that devastated her system.

Ecstasy roared through her and Zeke grew harder and bigger inside of her. And then he leaned over her, his hand still over her mouth, and he bit into her shoulder to silence his own cries as he exploded inside of her. She felt the powerful jets of semen against her inner walls, and it triggered another small orgasm that left her gasping for air.

Seconds, or minutes, or hours passed. She had no idea how long they lay there like that—him covering her body, his cock still semi-hard inside of her. She'd be sore. Eventually. But at the moment she could barely form a coherent thought in her head and her body was numb.

He kissed her shoulder—a sweet gesture considering the feralness of their lovemaking. And then he said something that would've made her laugh if she'd had the energy.

"If we hurry home we can do this again."

"As long as I don't have to do anything but lie there," she murmured, slurring her words like a drunk.

He slapped her ass and she gasped as he pulled out of her, the muscles of her vagina swollen and not wanting to release him. "And that's different how? You just laid there this time."

"If I had the energy I'd punch you for that."

"If you've got enough energy to punch me then you've got enough energy to be on top next time. Now pull your pants up and let's go or I'll throw you over my shoulder like you are and carry you out."

She wouldn't have put it past him, so she did as he asked.

Chapter Seven

Mia was half asleep as they parked the 4x4 in her spot, but movement near the stairs of her apartment caught her eye. Cooper was just coming down the stairs.

"I thought I'd take the chance y'all would be home," he said once they'd gotten out of the car.

Mia pulled her jacket tighter around her ripped shirt and wondered if she looked like she felt—like she'd been completely and satisfactorily fucked.

"What's up?" Zeke asked. "Come on in. We went to Duffey's for a couple beers."

To her surprise, Mia felt heat rise to her cheeks, and she was grateful it was dark.

"I'm surprised he even let you in the door," Cooper said, smiling. "Man, those were the days."

"I know. Whoever thought either of us would end up on the side of law and order?"

"Not Duffey, that's for damned sure."

Mia unlocked the door and shivered as a blast of cold wind wrapped around her porch, and then they all stepped inside into the warmth.

"I won't stay long," Cooper said. "I wanted to let you know a couple of fishermen found a body out where they were casting. She'd been in the water a couple days, but the coroner was able to ID her from her prints. She's identified as Tina Wolfe and has a record. Prostitution and petty theft for the most part. And she's associated with The Vaqueros. She was a house mouse for a while and then moved up to old lady status. She belonged to Wild Bill Jones."

"What was cause of death?" Zeke asked.

There was something in the tone of his voice that made her turn and look at him. And then everything started to fall into place and she knew.

"Her tongue was cut out and her hands were both cut off. And they branded her on the inside of her thigh. They're obviously sending a message. She ratted them out somehow." Cooper looked at Zeke with some kind of silent communication and she remembered Cooper wasn't a fool. He'd done his time in the military and a stint or two undercover as well. "Cause of death was a single gunshot wound to the head. Execution style. Just like The Vaqueros like. Just thought you might like to know."

"Yeah," Zeke said, nodding. "Thanks."

Cooper left and she closed and locked the door behind him. And then she turned around to face Zeke. "Tina Wolfe was your informant?" she asked.

He nodded and then paced to the wall and back, running his hands over the top of his head in frustration. "Son of a bitch."

The waves of his anger were palpable, and she knew if he had something to punch he would have. He'd take responsibility for Tina's death. Blame himself. That part hadn't changed. He'd always felt a personal responsibility—whether it was to the lowest kind of informant or one of his undercover officers. Everyone was *his*. He cared. Too deeply sometimes, and that's why he'd had such a hard time walking away from the job.

"She came in the shop last week," Mia said. She understood now. Knew why he'd been holding things back from her. He was working an op and he'd been using Tina to gather intel.

"I know," he said. "Just like I know you've got the music box. I snooped through your bag the other night while you were asleep."

Her lips pressed together, but she couldn't be mad. She'd have done the same thing if their positions had been reversed.

"I knew I could trust you with the information that's hidden in that music box. So I told Tina to be patient and wait, and then to take it from Wild Bill when she could. He's the club president and she was given a certain amount of freedom that the other women didn't have. She waited until they were gone to a club meeting and then took the music box. She told the other girls she was heading out to get her nails done. And she never looked back once she hit the road.

"She contacted me immediately. We told her we'd bring her in for protection if she brought us the box, but she didn't trust cops. Some habits die hard, and she felt she'd be safer on her own. So we had to come up with another plan. I gave her the address for your shop and told her to sell it to you and only you. She was determined to escape, despite the danger she knew she was in."

"That's a brave thing for a twenty-six-year-old woman to do. Especially one that's been trained to that kind of lifestyle, where she's taught early on that she has no independence or choices. The club's will is her will," Mia said.

"She was different," Zeke agreed. "Had backbone. And plans. She'd known from the start she'd work her way up, get some cash here and there on the side, and then move on. Neither of us saw it ending like this. She never made it to the checkpoint site. I knew that meant she was dead. I just didn't want to face it."

"I'm sorry, Zeke. I know it never gets easier."

"You almost get numb to it. And that's a dangerous thing."

"How'd you know I'd keep it?" she asked. "That's a hell of a risk to take on a hunch."

"I've always known you, Mia. Better than you know

yourself. I knew you'd want it for your own. You had a collection of antique jewelry boxes in our apartment. And if all else failed, I knew you'd never sell it back to the biker just out of principle. It's that intrinsic sense of justice you have. If you hadn't taken it for yourself, you would've saved it for some kid or some older woman who needed a special birthday gift for her granddaughter but didn't have a lot of budget."

"I don't like being pegged so easily," she said.

"You're a big softy, Mia Russo. And everybody knows it. It's why I'm glad you left the job when you did. It would've eventually broken you completely. You're not able to cut off your emotions and compartmentalize as well as some of us."

She frowned, thinking it was a criticism.

"That's a good thing, babe. It's what made you so good at your job. But it's what tore you up too. We can't save everyone."

"Would it help if I told you that about Tina?" she asked.

His smile was pensive. "No, I guess not. That's part of the job too. We think we can save everyone. And when we can't it's a hard dose of reality not easily accepted."

"You've gotten very philosophical in your old age."

"I think you just learn to appreciate what's important in life the older you get."

The way he looked at her made her feel like he was looking at her through a microscope. Like he could see her wants and fears and dreams. And that she loved him still. It was a distinctly uncomfortable feeling so she turned away and tried to find something to do with her hands.

Her gaze caught on her backpack that was still propped on the floor, and she went over to it and pulled out the wrapped box. She hadn't had the chance to look at it herself. Zeke had ears like a fox, and if she'd tried to wake up in the middle of the night to look at it, he'd have heard her. She took it to the table and unwrapped it, and then set it on the table gently.

"What was in it?" she asked.

"It was a recipe for a new amphetamine. It's not

controlled by the USFDA and it's not considered an illegal substance. You heard about the raids down in Wyoming?" he asked.

"As much as anyone. I try not to watch the news anymore."

"Consider yourself lucky. The Vaqueros opened fire on a restaurant on a Friday night after work. All in all, twenty-eight people were killed and a man name Joaquin Rivera was kidnapped. He was a scientist for the Del Fuego cartel before they were disbanded, and then one of the other cartels bought him because he's a very brilliant man with a twisted mind. He just happened to be in the United States visiting his sister, and The Vaqueros took full advantage of his visit. They tortured the recipe from him, shot him in the head, and brought it back to their territory here for their own cooks to experiment with."

"It would be worth millions on the open market."

"I know. But now we have it, thanks to Tina. And thanks to you. As far as we know this is the only copy."

"So that's the real reason you came to Surrender," she said. "Why didn't you just tell me the truth? I would've helped had I known."

"Because that's not the main reason I came to Surrender. It would've been much more convenient to set her up with a pawnshop a hundred miles away where our office is located. I came for you. Because I was tired of living without you. And anger and hurt can only carry a person so far before there's nothing left but emptiness.

"We made our mistakes, Mia. Both of us. I was too driven and you were afraid. And the timing wasn't right. But that doesn't mean we weren't right. My feelings for you have never changed. I went through phases where I wanted to blame you— hate you—but I couldn't because that would be like blaming myself—hating myself. And I didn't have the guts to live with that. Because you were the very best part of me."

She stared at him, her eyes pooling with tears, but they never fell. Panic enveloped him as she stayed silent and wrapped her arms around herself protectively. Couldn't she see she was holding his heart? He was giving her everything he had. And the promise of the man he wanted to be for her.

"What will it take, Mia? I don't have to take the job in Carson. I've been offered several administrative positions. Hell, I was even offered the chance to teach criminal justice classes at Declan College. Riley MacKenzie recommended me to the Dean. I don't have to be a cop. I love it. But it doesn't define me. All I know is that I'll do whatever it takes to be with you. What do you say? Can we give this a shot for real this time?"

* * * *

Mia felt numb on the inside—paralyzed by his words. For the first time in as long as she could remember the right thing to say wasn't waiting to roll off her tongue. Her vocal cords were frozen and she didn't seem to have any control over her emotions because she could've sworn she felt a tear slide down her cheek.

"Baby, you're killing me," he said. "Is the thought of spending your life with me that repulsive? I've never seen you speechless." He tried to smile but she could see he didn't quite have the ability to make it believable. He was serious. And she was terrified.

She opened her mouth to speak but nothing came out. Frustrated, she swiped the tear away from her cheek and wiped her hand on her jeans.

"Listen, we can take things slow," he said, rushing to speak to fill the silence. "I was going to buy a place here in Surrender. I like it here and it's an easy commute no matter where I decide to take a job. I was hoping it would be our home together, but we can live apart. You said we missed the dating stage. Now's our chance to make up for all that."

She wiped another tear away and laughed. The sound was rough and foreign, but at least she'd gotten something out. "Seven years too late," she said and watched his face fall into that empty mask he adopted whenever he didn't want someone to know if he was hurt.

And then she moved into him, wrapping her arms around him and crushing her mouth against his. He lifted her and she wrapped her legs around him, and then she leaned back and looked into his eyes.

"We're long past the dating stage," she said, rubbing her thumb along the edge of his beard. "Don't make me wait any longer for you. I've wanted you for an eternity." Her lips twitched and she said, "Maybe we can be grownups this time and have a serious relationship." She kissed him again and let her legs drop to the ground.

"Jesus, you scared the hell out of me."

"You took me by surprise. A part of me still thought you might leave."

He squeezed her tight and she could feel him shaking his head. "Such little faith. Don't worry, I'm sure I'll figure out some way to punish you."

"I can only imagine," she said, shivering against him at the thought of what was to come.

She looked him in the eyes, wanting him to know she spoke the truth. "Zeke, if you love being a cop then I want you to be a cop. Why would I ever ask you to do something you don't love? I love you too much to not want that for you. Whether you're back working patrol or you're sitting behind a desk. Make the choice. I'll love you any way."

The relief on his face told her she'd said the right thing. And she'd meant it. His happiness was as important as anything else. This time around they were going to put each other first and learn the value of compromise.

"If you don't like the house maybe we could keep living above the bakery for a while," he said. "I could get used to the smell of cinnamon rolls in the morning."

Mia moved in close so her breasts rubbed against him, and she nipped at his chest. "I could get used to having my way with you in the mornings."

His hands tangled in her hair and she leaned her head back so his lips could seek hers. "That's even better than cinnamon rolls," he whispered.

They were both laughing as he kissed her.

The End

If you enjoyed reading The Promise of Surrender, I would appreciate it if you would help others enjoy this book, too.

Lend it. This e-book is lending-enabled, so please, share it with a friend.

Recommend it. Please help other readers find this book by recommending it to friends, readers' groups and discussion boards.

Review it. Please tell other readers why you liked this book by reviewing it. Or visit me at http://www.lilianahart.com.

Join the Liliana Hart Newsletter!

WIN $100!

Beginning in April, I'll be giving away a $100 gift card* on the 15th of the month, and every month after, to one newsletter subscriber. The winner will be announced inside the newsletter, so you'll have to actually open it to see who won :-) So if you're not a newsletter subscriber, go do it. This will also be open to international readers.

*Must be deliverable online

Sign up for the 1001 Dark Nights Newsletter
and be entered to win a Tiffany Key necklace.

There's a contest every month!

Go to www.1001DarkNights.com to subscribe.

As a bonus, all subscribers will receive a free
1001 Dark Nights story
The First Night
by Lexi Blake & M.J. Rose

Turn the page for a full list of the
1001 Dark Nights fabulous novellas...

1001 Dark Nights

WICKED WOLF by Carrie Ann Ryan
A Redwood Pack Novella

WHEN IRISH EYES ARE HAUNTING by Heather Graham
A Krewe of Hunters Novella

EASY WITH YOU by Kristen Proby
A With Me In Seattle Novella

MASTER OF FREEDOM by Cherise Sinclair
A Mountain Masters Novella

CARESS OF PLEASURE by Julie Kenner
A Dark Pleasures Novella

ADORED by Lexi Blake
A Masters and Mercenaries Novella

HADES by Larissa Ione
A Demonica Novella

RAVAGED by Elisabeth Naughton
An Eternal Guardians Novella

DREAM OF YOU by Jennifer L. Armentrout
A Wait For You Novella

STRIPPED DOWN by Lorelei James
A Blacktop Cowboys ® Novella

RAGE/KILLIAN by Alexandra Ivy/Laura Wright
Bayou Heat Novellas

DRAGON KING by Donna Grant
A Dark Kings Novella

PURE WICKED by Shayla Black
A Wicked Lovers Novella

HARD AS STEEL by Laura Kaye
A Hard Ink/Raven Riders Crossover

STROKE OF MIDNIGHT by Lara Adrian
A Midnight Breed Novella

ALL HALLOWS EVE by Heather Graham
A Krewe of Hunters Novella

KISS THE FLAME by Christopher Rice
A Desire Exchange Novella

DARING HER LOVE by Melissa Foster
A Bradens Novella

TEASED by Rebecca Zanetti
A Dark Protectors Novella

THE PROMISE OF SURRENDER by Liliana Hart
A MacKenzie Family Novella

FOREVER WICKED by Shayla Black
A Wicked Lovers Novella

CRIMSON TWILIGHT by Heather Graham
A Krewe of Hunters Novella

CAPTURED IN SURRENDER by Liliana Hart
A MacKenzie Family Novella

SILENT BITE: A SCANGUARDS WEDDING
by Tina Folsom
A Scanguards Vampire Novella

DUNGEON GAMES by Lexi Blake
A Masters and Mercenaries Novella

AZAGOTH by Larissa Ione
A Demonica Novella

NEED YOU NOW by Lisa Renee Jones
A Shattered Promises Series Prelude

SHOW ME, BABY by Cherise Sinclair
A Masters of the Shadowlands Novella

ROPED IN by Lorelei James
A Blacktop Cowboys ® Novella

TEMPTED BY MIDNIGHT by Lara Adrian
A Midnight Breed Novella

THE FLAME by Christopher Rice
A Desire Exchange Novella

CARESS OF DARKNESS by Julie Kenner
A Dark Pleasures Novella

Also from Evil Eye Concepts:

TAME ME by J. Kenner
A Stark International Novella

THE SURRENDER GATE By Christopher Rice
A Desire Exchange Novel

SERVICING THE TARGET By Cherise Sinclair
A Masters of the Shadowlands Novel

Bundles:
BUNDLE ONE
Includes:
Forever Wicked by Shayla Black
Crimson Twilight by Heather Graham
Captured in Surrender by Liliana Hart
Silent Bite by Tina Folsom

BUNDLE TWO
Includes:
Dungeon Games by Lexi Blake
Azagoth by Larissa Ione
Need You Now by Lisa Renee Jones
Show My, Baby by Cherise Sinclair

BUNDLE THREE
Includes:
Roped In by Lorelei James
Tempted By Midnight by Lara Adrian
The Flame by Christopher Rice
Caress of Darkness by Julie Kenner

About Liliana Hart

Liliana Hart is a *New York Times*, *USA Today*, and Publisher's Weekly Bestselling Author of more than 40 titles. After starting her first novel her freshman year of college, she immediately became addicted to writing and knew she'd found what she was meant to do with her life. She has no idea why she majored in music.

Since self-publishing in June of 2011, Liliana has sold more than 4 million ebooks and been translated into eight languages. She's appeared at #1 on lists all over the world and all three of her series have appeared on the New York Times list. Liliana is a sought after speaker and she's given keynote speeches and self-publishing workshops to standing-room-only crowds from California to New York to London.

Liliana can almost always be found at her computer writing or on the road giving workshops for SilverHart International, a company she founded with her partner, Scott Silverii, where they provide law enforcement, military, and fire resources for writers so they can write it right. Liliana is a recent transplant to Southern Louisiana, where she's getting used to the humidity and hurricane season, and plotting murders (for her books, of course).

Connect with me online:
http://twitter.com/Liliana_Hart
http://facebook.com/LilianaHart
My Website: http://www.lilianahart.com

Captured in Surrender

A MacKenzie Family Novella
By Liliana Hart
Now Available

Bounty Hunter Naya Blade never thought she'd step foot in Surrender, Montana again. Especially since there was a warrant out for her arrest. But when her skip ends up in the normally peaceful town, she has no choice but to go after him to claim her reward. Even at the cost of running into the cop that makes her blood run hot and her sense of self-preservation run cold.

Deputy Lane Greyson wants to see Naya in handcuffs, but he'd much prefer them attached to his bed instead of in a cold jail cell. She drove him crazy once before and then drove right out of town, leaving havoc in her wake. He's determined to help her hunt down the bad guy so he can claim his own bounty—her.

* * * *

Lane knew the moment Naya had stepped back into his town. There was something about her that called to him, like she was a siren song and he couldn't help but answer.

It had been just over a year since he'd seen her last. Since she'd ridden into town on that wicked bike looking for her brother. Colton Blade had been in the military with Cooper MacKenzie, and he'd always told his sister that if he ever got into trouble, then Cooper was who he'd go to for help.

But Colt turned out to be a bad seed—alcohol, drugs, assault charges, bar fights...and attempted murder. Colt Blade was more trouble than he was worth in Lane's opinion—someone who'd been given too many second chances and pissed them all away. Naya knew it too. But she'd still come after him, hoping he'd listen to her when she asked him to go back and face trial.

Naya had found Cooper, hoping he'd seen or heard from her brother, but Cooper hadn't been in touch with Colt for more than a decade. Lane had just come in from lunch to see her standing there in the office, and despite her brave front, he'd seen the despair etched on her face.

The sight of her had been like a punch to the solar plexus. Her face was a study. It shouldn't have been beautiful—not if you looked at her features individually. Her face was angular and her cheekbones flat, attributing her Native American heritage. Her nose was long and straight and her chin slightly pointed. But her eyes were what made a man lose his mind—exotic in shape and the color of dark chocolate, fringed with full black lashes. Thick brows winged above them, giving her a perpetual look of challenge.

She was tall—close to six feet—and her jeans had hugged her curves in all the right places. The belly-baring top she'd worn had shown a pierced navel, and the muscles in her arms were sinewy and lean.

He'd been struck speechless at the sight of her, his cock going rock hard in an instant and the wild lust of need surging through his body like it never had before. He'd have done anything to keep her around longer, just to satisfy his curiosity and see if her lips were as soft as he imagined they were. To see if she felt the connection the same as he did. He'd seen the way her nipples had hardened when she turned her dark gaze on him.

It had been a no-brainer to volunteer to help her search for her brother. He'd done it as much for himself as for her.

He'd never believed in love at first sight, but the moment he'd met Naya, those beliefs had been reevaluated. Their chemistry had been palpable—a living, breathing thing. And the heat that sizzled between them was hot enough to singe anyone who got too close. He'd had no control over his body in that instant, and that's something that had never happened to him before.

It looked like things hadn't changed much. His dick was

hard enough to hammer nails and the feel of her against him, the challenge in her eyes daring him to do something about it, made him want to bend her over the bike, strip off those skin-tight jeans, and slide right between the creamy folds of her pussy.

"You're under arrest," he said instead, taking a step back so she couldn't feel his arousal. He didn't recognize the sound of his voice, the low rasp of desire.

"Oh, come on now, Deputy." Her lips quirked as if they were sharing a private joke. "That fight wasn't my fault, and I am hardly to blame for all the damage that was done. If you remember, I believe I was otherwise—" she took a step closer to him so her breasts rubbed against his arm, and she whispered the words so he felt them blow across his lips, "—occupied when the fight started."

She'd definitely been occupied. They'd been in one of the back rooms at Duffey's Bar. They'd started out doing body shots of tequila, getting more daring with each one. A lick of salt across the top of her breast before the shot was thrown back, burning the whole way down. Another lick low on his belly, so her cheek pressed against his hardness as she swiped with her tongue.

It hadn't taken long until she'd borrowed his handcuffs and latched him to the gold bar that rimmed the pool table. And then she'd knelt in front of him and taken every inch of his cock like it was her last meal.

He remembered the bite of her nails on his thighs and the way she stared up at him with those dark bedroom eyes— dreamed about it for the past year until his body was so hot and his cock so hard that he'd had no choice but to stroke himself to completion just so he could get some damn sleep.

Sweet Surrender

A MacKenzie Family Novella
By Liliana Hart
Coming December 13, 2016

It's been twelve years since Liza Carmichael stepped foot in Surrender, but after her great aunt's death she has no choice but to return and settle her estate. Which includes the corner bakery that's been a staple in Surrender for more than fifty years.

After twenty-five years on the job, Lieutenant Grant Boone finds himself at loose ends now that he's retired. He's gotten a number of job offers—one from MacKenzie Security—but he's burned out and jaded, and the last thing he wants to do is carry the burden of another badge and weapon. He almost turns down the invitation from his good friend Cooper MacKenzie to stay as their guest for a few weeks while he's deciding what to do with the rest of his life. But he packs his bag and heads to Surrender anyway.

The only thing Boone knows is that his future plans don't include Liza Carmichael. She's bossy, temperamental, and the confections she bakes are sweet enough to tempt a saint. Thank God he's never pretended to be one. But after he gets one taste of Liza and things start heating up in the kitchen, he realizes how delicious new beginnings can be.

MacKenzie Family World

Dear Readers,

I'm thrilled to be able to introduce the MacKenzie Family World to you. I asked five of my favorite authors to create their own characters and put them into the world you all know and love. These amazing authors revisited Surrender, Montana, and through their imagination you'll get to meet new characters, while reuniting with some of your favorites.

These stories are hot, hot, hot—exactly what you'd expect from a MacKenzie story—and it was pure pleasure for me to read each and every one of them and see my world through someone else's eyes. They definitely did the series justice, and I hope you discover five new authors to put on your auto-buy list.

Make sure you check out *Troublemaker,* a brand new, full-length MacKenzie novel written by me. And yes, you'll get to see more glimpses of Shane before his book comes out next year.

So grab a glass of wine, pour a bubble bath, and prepare to Surrender.

Love Always,

Liliana Hart

Coming February 16, 2016.

Desire & Ice by Christopher Rice
Bullet Proof by Avery Flynn
Deep Trouble by Kimberly Kincaid
Delta Rescue by Cristin Harber
Rush by Robin Covington
Trouble Maker by Liliana Hart

Welcome to Storm, Texas, where passion runs hot, desire runs deep, and secrets have the power to destroy...

Nestled among rolling hills and painted with vibrant wildflowers, the bucolic town of Storm, Texas, seems like nothing short of perfection.

But there are secrets beneath the facade. Dark secrets. Powerful secrets. The kind that can destroy lives and tear families apart. The kind that can cut through a town like a tempest, leaving jealousy and destruction in its wake, along with shattered hopes and broken dreams. All it takes is one little thing to shatter that polish.

Reading like an on-going drama in the tradition of classic day and night-time soap operas like Dallas, Dynasty, and All My Children, *Rising Storm* is full of scandal, deceit, romance, passion, and secrets.

With 1001 Dark Nights as the "producer," Julie Kenner and Dee Davis use a television model with each week building on the last to create a storyline that fulfills the promise of a drama-filled soap opera. Joining Kenner and Davis in the "writer's room" is an incredible group of *New York Times* bestselling authors such as Lexi Blake, Elisabeth Naughton, Jennifer Probst, Larissa Ione, Rebecca Zanetti and Lisa Mondello who have brought their vision of Storm to life.

A serial soap opera containing eight episodes in season one, the season premiere of *Rising Storm*, TEMPEST RISING, debuted September 24th with each subsequent episode released consecutively that fall.

So get ready. The storm is coming.
Experience Rising Storm At... http://risingstormbooks.com

On behalf of 1001 Dark Nights,
Liz Berry and M.J. Rose would like to thank ~

Steve Berry
Doug Scofield
Kim Guidroz
Jillian Stein
InkSlinger PR
Dan Slater
Asha Hossain
Chris Graham
Pamela Jamison
Jessica Johns
Dylan Stockton
Richard Blake
BookTrib After Dark
The Dinner Party Show
and Simon Lipskar

CPSIA information can be obtained
at www.ICGtesting.com
Printed in the USA
LVHW02s2012110518
576873LV00001B/52/P